SOMETHING'S GOING ON HERE

A FAREWELL TO HARM

By

Ruth Cherry, Ph. D.

EXPLORA BOOKS
700 – 838 West Hastings St. Vancouver, BC V6C 0A6
www. explorabooks.com
Phone: (604) 330 6795

ISBN: 978-1-998394-45-6

RUTH CHERRY, Ph.D

SOMETHING'S GOING ON HERE

A FAREWELL TO HARM

"*Eloquent and smooth, deftly engulfing...*"

A PSYCHOLOGICAL THRILLER

Table of Contents

CHAPTER 1

<u>A Farewell to Harm</u>

If you didn't know any better, you'd think it was just another grey misty Friday morning in Los Osos, a quaint costal town in central California… But my name is Nick Sanders and *I do* know better.

I sit in my usual booth at Cad's coffee shop, the brim of my beat up Phillies cap pulled low to hide my face, sipping on my usual hot beverage with trembling hands and reflecting on how unusual my life has become since I moved to this godforsaken place.

Barely three months ago I was down on all fours plucking shards of broken window glass from the floor of my long term rental house, just your average retired Penn State English professor tidying up after helping a joint task-force take down an international crime ring trafficking super-marijuana from the U.S. into Mexico and putting one of the world's most influential men behind bars.

By that point I had already been shunned by most of the town, my life threatened so many times that I'd lost count. And these were not idle threats either mind you… My car had been blown up, my skull cracked open like an egg, and a rock had been thrown through my window. Twice.

But the worst thing that happened, the absolute worst thing that has happened to me by far, didn't actually happen to me. It happened to my beloved black lab Hildy, who I found pinned to my bedroom wall with a sword, the words "You're Next" written in blood next to her dangling body.

After all the insanity and heartbreak, I went through in such a short amount of time it was only natural to be confident I would finally prevail over what is usually considered a storyteller's greatest foe; the dreaded writer's block...

But month went by and I was still staring at the blank page on the screen of a laptop.

I had borrowed from my cousin Ellie... All of the notes I had excitedly scribbled down in preparation for my magnum opus, my Ulysses, were staring up at me from a bright yellow legal pad, mocking my hubris.

It looked like, for the time being anyway, the only story I would be telling would be to myself. And I'd already heard it all before.

When the phone rang that morning I actually welcomed the interruption, glad for the distraction. Maybe it was The President calling to commend me on a job well done. Once a writer always a writer. We dream big.

But it was not the President. "I will hunt you down, and I will kill you." Those were Chase Slate's exact words to me. To say that I was stunned would be an understatement along the lines of describing water as wet, or that Henry VIII really liked getting married. Los Osos means 'the bears' in Spanish, and I had woken the biggest and meanest one from hibernation and roused it from its cave, however that didn't mean I now had to fall to the ground and play dead.

After trying a breathing exercise my estranged wife Rosemary had taught me I had calmed my nerves enough to go fishing in the drawer of my nightstand, sighing with relief when I found what I was looking for - A folded up piece of paper

Marco had slipped to me as we said our goodbyes and he made his way back home to Mexico.

I was in the process of dialing the number he had written down when my front door swung open and there stood my cousin Ellie, tears streaming down her face. "Chase… He escaped."

That was yesterday. Yesterday I was stronger, ready to face whatever came next. Today, practically cowering in the back booth of this coffee shop, I'm not too sure that's still the case.

I'm not a gambling man, but if I was, I would be willing to bet that the odds of me seeing my next birthday have gone down significantly in the last 24 hours. Maybe they've been gradually going down from the moment my now deceased 1998 Honda Civic crossed the city limits, plummeting on that fatefully night not too long ago when I decided to go for a stroll one foggy evening and heard a gunshot ring out in the dark.

I look up when the bell above the entrance dings. It's my cousin Ellie, walking into the coffee shop dressed like a character out of a 1950s spy movie. Half her face is hidden behind Oliver Goldsmith Manhattan sunglasses and the other half under a wide brimmed hat, a dark scarf wrapped twice around her neck for good measure.

I can't help but chuckle at her "disguise", not necessarily at its theatricality, but more her logic that no one here would recognize a prominent real estate agent whose face is on multiple park benches in a town she's lived in half her life. She's probably sold most of the people in this room their homes for crying out loud!

I love my cousin dearly. She's a very smart and capable woman, albeit a little pushy at times, and occasionally prone to hyperbole. If I'm being honest a part of me blames her for this mess we're all in right now. She was the one who convinced

me to leave behind a meticulously crafted if somewhat lonely life of structure and order to move out west. When this whole thing started, she and best friend Deb pretty much bullied me into "asking around" town to get to the truth of it all, setting me on a collision course with the dark underbelly of Los Osos, a journey of fire and pain that would fundamentally alter me forever, a path with no end yet in sight. Conversely, I'm also grateful to her for mostly the same reasons.

My thoughts linger on Deb as they often do when I think back on those early days of intrigue. Poor sweet Deb. Was she truly destined to die of a brain embolism as Chase had so casually informed me? I try not to indulge in that kind of thinking, regret is a rabbit hole I wander down often enough as it is. She was a good friend. I feel her spirit with me always.

I'm not a particularly spiritual person, that was more of Rosemary's thing. On most days I do believe in a higher power though, a divine architect to hold accountable for fashioning the universe and molding us irresponsible mortals from stardust. I still miss her, but not as much as I used to because of one specific reason, and that reason has just walked through the door alongside my cousin.

Lauren, my would-be coconut scented muse, the prospective Nora Barnacle to my potential James Joyce. If anyone can jumpstart my imagination and get the creative juices flowing, surely it's her.

We've been inseparable ever since her children left to spend the summer with their father in Colorado. She doesn't care if I'm a balding academic with neurotic tendencies that trouble seems to follow around like a tail. Which is why she isn't safe here. None of us are. Not with Chase on the loose and looking to exact who knows what kind of dastardly revenge upon me.

I wave them over, making room for Lauren beside me while Ellie slides in right across. The first thing I do is tell them both I'm sorry. My love has put them in the crosshairs of a madman. Ellie looks almost embarrassed to acknowledge my apology (we Maltese are a curious people), while Lauren smiles and squeezes my hand reassuringly. "It's not your fault. None of this is your fault."

"Wait. Where are your suitcases?" I ask in a panic, suddenly afraid that I could be traveling alone.

"Relax. They're in my SUV." Ellie answers. "So you're sure we have to leave? Can't Les…"

I waste no time interrupting her. "The sheriff is useless, Cuz. You know that. He's too old to care, and too stubborn to retire." "And Marco? Can we trust him?" Lauren asks, narrowing

her eyes suspiciously.

I shrug. "More than we can trust our own government it looks like. There's no way Chase escaped without inside help." Lauren nods her agreement. "Did you talk to Maddy yet?

She's in as much danger as the rest of us."

"I tried. Explained the whole situation to her and everything. But you know Maddy… nothing scares her." I shake my head in frustration, yet there are hints of admiration and envy in my voice.

Ellie bangs her fist on the table like a gavel. "That's that then. Looks like we're heading to Mexico."

"Looks like." I mumble, mostly to myself, as I raise my mug in a halfhearted farewell to Cads, and by extension, Los Osos.

Lauren stands. "What are we waiting for then? Let's vamoose!" She declares in butchered Spanish.

I grab my duffle bag from under the table, a tad despondent as I realize how much of my life I am able to fit into such a receptacle as I follow the women out to the parking lot.

As we pile into Ellie's SUV Maddy comes wheeling down the sidewalk to see us off, lambasting all the fleeing pedestrians for being in her way. I ask if she would reconsider coming with us, but she scoffs at the idea of leaving Los Osos. I'm almost worried for her, but she's a tough old bird and I suspect I should be more afraid for anyone who means to do her harm.

Sunlight bursts through the clouds as we drive past the 'Welcome to Los Osos' sign on the edge of town, as if the climate itself was happy to see us go. I realize I might actually miss this strange little corner of the world. But then I look up at the rearview mirror and see a plume of black smoke peeking above the tree line, and I intuitively know that the rental house I reluctantly called home is currently burning to the ground.

Now that I'm actually thinking about it all, it actually *is* just another day in Los Osos, where the weather can turn on you almost as quickly as its eccentric residents, and dangerous people lurk around every corner.

As I settle in for the long trip I assure myself that Mexico is nice this time of year, and even if it isn't, it can't be worse than here…

CHAPTER 2
The Odyssey

We have been on the road for almost three days, staying at cheap motels, living off of vending machine chocolate bars and stale soda pop, and somewhere between Trail Rider's Inn in Tombstone and the Apache Motel in Alamogordo, uncertainty and boredom had begun to take its toll.

We are somewhere outside of Roswell on the edge of the New Mexico desert when Ellie and Lauren start to turn on each other. If I hadn't been so busy looking out the window for flying saucers maybe I would have seen the signs. Or maybe I had been privy to them all along and simply chose to bury my head in the proverbial desert sand that is my second brain.

On long stretches of highway with nothing to see for miles in any direction but each other's faces, the SUV slowly becomes a prison on wheels. Silly things as arbitrary as who gets to pick the music become power struggles between my cousin and my Lauren (To label her as my girlfriend just feels rude at this point.), a battle of wills in an effort to assert some kind of control in a situation that we would be fools to think we have any influence over. In the world outside the SUV there is a very powerful psychopath who wants my head on a platter, but here, inside this vehicle, here they can at least pretend to be the captains of their own destiny. I however, am under no such illusions.

I took a northern route the last time I drove across this vast expanse, keeping to major highways and roads for expediency. All this big sky country is new to me, and I can't help but relish every moment. Who wouldn't want to see where Wyatt Earp and his brothers took on the Cochise County Cowboys during the famous gunfight at the O.K. Corral? Or the site of the Trinity Tests where the very first atomic bomb was detonated? I was experiencing America on a visceral level, like Lewis & Clark before me but in reverse. I guess it's true what some champion race car driver once said - The closer you are to death the more alive you feel.

Ellie's voice cuts through my meandering thoughts like a knife through melting butter. "Hey! What was wrong with that one?!" She exclaims as Lauren changes the station without warning yet again.

"It was fine… If you like that sort of Yacht rock stuff." Lauren replies snootily, still fidgeting with the radio dial.

"Well it's my car, and I happen to think that Christopher Cross is the pinnacle of modern American music!" Ellie shoots back angrily, swatting Lauren's interloping hand away.

"What do you think, Nick?" They ask in unison without even turning to look at me as I mind my own business in the back seat.

I try not to take the bait, not to come down on either side of this tug of war. I honestly have no strong opinions on the subject one way or the other,. But since I'm me and I can't help but charge headlong into trouble, I offer up the only compromise I can think of. "Maybe we can find a station playing some Bob Dylan?

Ellie holds nothing back. "Are you kidding me? Dylan was a rambling buffoon."

Lauren nods enthusiastically and chimes in. "Couldn't agree more. He thought he was such a cool cat but he was nothing more than a bargain bin poet with mediocre guitar strumming." I bristle somewhat at their simplistic assessment of a treasured American folk singer, but it seems my job here is done. I have successfully, albeit unintentionally, managed to unite my two favorite people against a common foe - My taste in music.

Exchanges like this will continue to pepper our trip until we get to the next motel, heated verbal ping pong matches where the only things at stake are our sanity and civility, and the questionable disdain for a folk music icon. But for the time being all is well in the kingdom of Ellie's SUV.

I sigh as I lean my head against the window, reminding myself how much I love these two women as I watch the clouds drift like lumbering buffalo across the windswept mesa.

CHAPTER 3

<u>Crossing Over To The Other Side</u>

I am wandering barefoot across an arid landscape of flaxen sand and jagged rock, ripples of intense heat wafting above the scattered patches of cacti and agave all the way to a burning orange horizon.

My throat is dry, my face is numb, and I am well past the point of delirium as the vultures circle above, eagerly waiting for me to drop dead from dehydration.

It would be so much easier to give up rather than to go on. I am Atlas carrying the weight of the entire world on my shoulders. I am Sisyphus pushing my boulder up a mountain, knowing it will only roll back down to the bottom every time I reach the summit.

I am Jesus fasting in the desert and the devil walks beside me, tempting me to cast my burdens aside and lay down in the dirt; to close my eyes and wait for the winged scavengers to swoop in and feast on me until my bones are picked clean, left to bleach under the punishing sun as a warning to all the wayward travelers who will come after.

But I spy a reprieve in the distance, hope in the form of a shimmering oasis nestled along the banks of the Rio Grande. Is this real or is it simply a beautiful mirage conjured up by my dying brain to coax me across the veil of eternal sleep? I decide that I don't care. I am irresistibly drawn to it, whatever it may turn out to be.

And so I trudge across the withering arroyo, headlong through an unforgiving landscape infested with scorpions and snakes and all other manner of deadly creepy crawlies. Over steep embankments and down rocky crags, no matter how difficult the terrain, I do not give up until the burning sand turns to cool grass beneath the soles of my feet.

I have arrived with my lungs on fire, every tortured muscle in my body screaming with joy as I fall to my knees at the edge of paradise, too distracted to notice the rattlesnake coiled by my blistered feet. It hisses up at me, its forked tongue flicking in and out of its scaly mouth like a centipede. The final obstacle in my journey. The demon guarding the way back into Eden… I slowly start to move away, but this only serves to aggravate the snake even further. It tenses up, ready to strike. Yet to my surprise I am somehow able to catch it by its neck as it lashes out at me, its fangs just inches from my face, dripping with venom.

I frantically pat the ground around me with my free hand, finding a rock slightly larger than my fist within reach. I muster up the last of my strength and pin the snake to the grass, savagely bashing its head in until only the bloody stump remains. I am not Moses. I have come too far for my story to end with the promised land just within my reach.

The rattle of danger now extinguished, I hear the rush of water just beyond a lush thicket and I waste no time blundering through the foliage, barely feeling the branches clawing at my skin. I come out on the other side and I can barely believe my

eyes, my mouth agape as I stare in awe at the bend of the grand river as it curves inward before me.

I tear off my clothes excitedly, plunging straight into its sparkling waters, greedily drinking as I wade deeper into its welcoming embrace. I dive underwater, with no intention of resurfacing until all of my transgressions are washed away.

When I finally do come up for air I see my beloved Hildy on the opposite side of the river bank, her tail wagging as she laps up the refreshing water. I am overjoyed to see her looking so young and vibrant, the healthy sheen of her black coat positively lustrous in the sunlight. I come to the happy conclusion that all dogs do go to heaven after all.

Our reunion is abruptly cut short when I see the leaves behind the dog rustle. We are not alone. There is a large shape moving stealthily through the bushes, a predator stalking its prey. I try to warn Hildy by yelling out her name, but for some reason she cannot hear me. I splash around in the water, haplessly trying to get her attention. In the end all I can do is watch as the mountain lion pounces, ripping my poor dog to shreds right before my very eyes.

The beast has killed for pleasure, not out of necessity, and when it is done mauling my sweet Hildy it turns its gaze upon me, hungrily licking its bloodstained muzzle, almond eyes glinting with menace.

I turn and swim back toward muddy banks Rio Grande, hearing a loud splash as the big cat jumps in to give chase…

I awaken with a sharp gasp, startling poor Lauren, who is behind the wheel of the SUV.

"Jeez. Everything okay back there, hun? Did you have a bad dream?" She asks with concern. "Are we there yet?" I ask groggily and Ellie chuckles without taking her eyes off the game she is playing on her phone.

"Nope. Still in Texas." Lauren offers. "You've been asleep since we left the motel in San Antonio."

I sit up and look out the window just as we pass a ridiculously large Texaco gas station. Everything is bigger in Texas I think to myself, including my nightmares.

"I can't believe you didn't wake me when we passed the Alamo." I say crabbily.

"I tried to." She grumbles sourly. "You just mumbled something about being Jesus and went back to snoring. I didn't know you were religious…"

"I'm not." I counter. "But I'm starting to suspect that my subconscious might be."

CHAPTER 4

Adios Tejas, ¡Hola! Mexico

According to the GPS on the SUV's dashboard we are approximately 30 minutes away from the border crossing, cruising down State Highway 255 just above the speed limit, bypassing downtown Laredo altogether.

Frankly I'm a little disappointed at this information. If you ask me we Americans spend too much time traversing the country on interstates and highways, skirting past the small towns and sacrificing the actual Americana of it all in the name of convenience and expediency.

An 18-wheeler roars past us, kicking up a cloud of dust in its wake, and I can't help but romanticize the life of the long haul trucker that I imagine is behind the wheel. His name is Magnus, and he has a beautiful wife and two kids (one that he suspects isn't his) waiting for him back in Minnesota. He has spent the last week eroding the inner lining of his stomach with strong coffee and his sciatica is acting up. He is the unsung hero of an increasingly callous and jaded nation Why can I only write like this in my head?

Ellie turns up the music to drown out the outside noise of trucks zooming past us as we near the Laredo–Colombia Solidarity International Bridge; massive land whales transporting everything from television sets to boxes of breakfast cereal and congesting the eight lane structure built above the muddy waters of the Rio Grande.

It takes us the better half of an hour to get to the checkpoint where a Mexican immigration officer asks to see our passports. She stamps Lauren's and Ellie's without issue, but I frown when she takes mine into her booth, realizing something must be up when picks up the phone on her desk…

After an uncomfortable amount of time and a cacophony of honking horns, a Mexican soldier with a Colt 9mm SMG strapped to his chest waves us over to the shoulder, giving way to the torrent of the vehicles that have piled up behind us.

A dusty white SUV with a pine green stripe down both its back doors pulls up alongside ours, and a short man in a plaid shirt and a wide brimmed cowboy hat hops out of the vehicle. He walks over to the driver's side of our car at a brisk pace and taps his badge on the window.

"What's going on here, cuz?" Ellie asks me in a panic. "I'm… I… I'm not really sure." I stammer.

"What should I do, Nick?" Lauren asks as the man's taping becomes more urgent.

"We've got no choice. Roll down the window and see what he wants." I finally answer, hoping that this isn't some kind of shakedown.

Lauren presses the button on her armrest and the car window inches down, its leisurely pace only adding to my growing anxiety. I've read horror stories on the internet about this sort of thing but I never thought it could happen to me.

"Are you Nick Sanders and la compañía?" The man inquires in a thick sing-song accent. "Who wants to know?" I ask from the back seat, my fists balled up so tightly my knuckles blanch.

"My name is Augusto Rivera. I am here on the behalf of *La Policía Federal*." He answers curtly. "You are all to follow me now. Come this way please." He adds, his politeness purely perfunctory.

He opens Lauren's door, practically yanking her out of the car. Terrified into compliance, she looks back at me as he leads her by the wrist toward the white SUV. "Nick, honey? I'm I being abducted?"

"It's okay, honey. Let's just do what the nice men with the guns tell us to and I'm sure everything will be okay." I reply, not knowing what else to say.

"I can't just leave my truck here! It's a lease!" Ellie complains, pounding on the shoulders of a young soldier as scoops her out of the passenger seat.

Knowing that resistance is futile, I hold up my hands and exit the car of my own volition, following after Lauren and Ellie without objection as our luggage is ferried to the trunk of the White SUV.

I get into the car, Ellie shooting daggers at me as I smoosh up against her in the cramped back seat. Augusto, riding shotgun, turns to us and smiles. "I'm sorry for the, *como que*, how you can say *el teatro* in English? I'm sorry for the acting. Inside here now you can know that Marco has sent me. Welcome to México, mis amigos!" He declares as he laughs.

It takes a minute for his words to register, but when they do we all start laughing along with him, all the tension melting away like a popsicle in a heatwave.

"I knew it." I blurt out, more to myself than as a direct response to the revelation. "I knew we were okay!"

"Oh you did, did you?" Ellie jibes. "That pee stain on the front of your pants says otherwise."

I look down and she flicks up my nose. Older cousins are great that way. "So what will happen to my car?" Ellie asks between chuckles.

Augusto's face suddenly turns serious. "*Que claro*, we shall strip it for the parts and then set fire to what remains."

Ellie's face whitens with alarm but the federale smiles again, with the soldier behind the wheel cracking a smile as he shakes his head. "It's only a joke, *tia. No seas tan seria*. Did you really believe my joke? You watch too many Hollywood movies. Your Ford is safe at the border. My cousin will look after it."

After our nervous giggles have died down, Augusto sets a brown paper box on the center console . "Please deposit your mobile phones here please."

I drop mine in without a second thought, I have gone this long without the trappings of 21st century technology in my life, what's another few weeks?

But Ellie protests. "Wait! I need to call my girlfriend and let her know that am I okay!" "And I need to be able to talk to my children!" Lauren chimes in.

"I am sorry, *mis amigas*, Mexico has many eyes and ears that are too easily for sale. For you to be safe, *El Diablo Blanco* must not discover where you are going. I am certain Marco has made it possible for you to contact the loved ones you have left behind when the time is good." Augusto says with confidence, assuaging current fears while rekindling old ones, specifically that Chase is still out there and his reach is far…

Lauren looks to Ellie, who nods in resignation as she powers down her phone and drops it in the box.

"I better be able to call my kids at some point." Lauren threatens as she follows suit.

The White SUV drives through an open chain link gate right onto the tarmac of a small airfield where a Robinson R44 four-seat light helicopter is waiting, its rotors whirling and ready for takeoff.

Before I follow Lauren and Ellie to the chopper I turn to Augusto and shake his hand. "Thank you for everything. If you're ever where we're heading I'd like to buy you a drink of tequila."

"*Via con dios, Nicolás.* I am sure we shall see each other again." He promises.

"Do you know happen to know where this bird taking us?" I ask, ever curious.

"To paradise, *mis amigo.* To paradise." He assures me with a smile.

CHAPTER 5

I Can See Cuba From My Safe House

Our cramped helicopter hems_close to the coastline as we soar over the Gulf of Mexico, casting a shadow down upon miles and miles of uninterrupted virgin beach snaking along an emerald ocean. I am sitting up in the front of the cockpit, my face pressed against the stretched-acrylic glass hatch like a child in the back of a station wagon, taking everything in.

Despite the low grade neophobia that was endemic to my life before I moved to Los Osos, this isn't my first time out of the United States (although you wouldn't know it from the goofy smile on my face right now). Throughout the years I have attended the occasional academic conference in such countries as Canada, Germany, and England. But the difference between those trips and this latest excursion outside of my comfort zone is that back then I didn't have much interest in exploration for explorations sake, only leaving the hotels where the conferences were being held to return to the airport. I regret being so closed off to new experiences now.

These last few months of living on the edge of a knife have made me realize just how little life experiences I had.

Also, the cities of Ontario, Hannover, and London, while impressive and beautiful in their own right (from what little I saw anyway), are decidedly metropolitan. Whereas the appeal of the tropical playground sprawled out around us is its promise of a decidedly different sort of adventure.

The pilot informs me that we are now entering Quintana Roo, a Mexican state located on the easternmost tip of the Yucatán Peninsula and only 120 miles from Cuba. It would have taken us 30 hours by car, but up here in this bird, we've managed to make the trip in a fraction of that time.

I don't think I would have minded the drive though, being down there amongst it all, immersing myself in the country's rich culture. Strolling through cobblestone towns in a Hawaiian shirt and ogling the Spanish built churches like a tourist while eating palm sized tacos or grilled corn garnished with chili powder, cheese, and lime. No, I don't think I would have minded at all.

The closer we get to the airport the more civilization creeps back in to reassert its dominance over the land, and the untouched beaches gradually giving way to one seaside resort hotel after another, with massive multilevel cruise ships buoyed in the Riviera Maya like floating cities.

We land away from the main terminals, next to a large commercial aviation warehouse, and I am relieved to see that Marco is there to meet us. I'm not sure if I can call us friends exactly; perhaps our relationship would be best described as soldiers (reluctant in my case) who have been through battle together. That kind of shared ordeal tends to forge a strong bond between two people, a bond that is not easily forgotten nor broken.

"Welcome to Tulum, Nick. It's good to see you." He says, clasping my forearm just below the elbow.

"I really appreciate what you're doing for us, Marco. You're literally saving our lives." I reply, unsure how I will ever be able to proportionally express my gratitude.

Marco nods at Lauren and Ellie. "Ladies. Come. We must not linger here, compadre. Andale. Follow me." He says, beckoning us over to a black government issue SUV parked in a hangar.

Thirty minutes later and that same black SUV is streaking down Carretera Federal 307 with us in it. If there is a speed limit on this highway then we are a exempt, whizzing past billboards advertising beach resorts and restaurants in nearby Playa del Carmen, and the cenote (cavern) tours and Mayan ruins that Tulum is known for.

I am looking forward to finally seeing my first Mexican town when the driver suddenly makes a hard left, turning off the main highway onto a gravel road a few miles short of the town center.

We pass tourists cycling in the direction of all the beachfront resorts peeking up behind the palm trees in the distance, as well as locals in various colored polo shirts paired with khaki shorts, employees on their way to and from work at those same resorts. The long road ends at the guardhouse of a gated community, and when Marco rolls down the window to show the sentry his badge, I smell the sea.

I don't know what I was expecting in a safe house, but it certainly wasn't a three story, six-bedroom art deco villa by the ocean with a fully stocked kitchen and bar, a swimming pool, and a hot tub on the roof.

"Say hello to your new home, compadres." Marco says, quite satisfied with himself.

"Marco, how did you arrange all of this?" Lauren asks in disbelief.

"We seized this property from one of the cartel bosses last week as part of an ongoing investigation. It's all yours for as long as you need it." He explains while sliding open the glass doors that lead out onto the patio.

We follow him out to the beach, removing our shoes so that we can dig our toes into the sand as we take in the impossibly gorgeous view.

Welcome to Tulum indeed - Where the vast sky meets a grand ocean, and the turquoise water is always 75 degrees and waist deep due to the peninsula's proximity to the Mesoamerican Barrier Reef System.

"Hey, is that Cuba?" I ask excitedly, pointing to a sliver of grey wedged into the horizon.

Marco squints his eyes and chuckles. "I think that's an oil tanker."

"Yeah, of course. I knew that." I retort in an attempt to salvage some dignity, pretending I notice something further down the beach.

"Let's get a drink." Marco suggests. "Would anyone like a piña colada?"

"Is a frog's butt watertight?" Ellie answers colorfully, following Marco back to the house.

I smile and take Lauren's hand, giving it a little squeeze. We spend the next few minutes watching the sun's reflection stretch out on the water as it dips behind our safe house.

I don't believe in fate. It's been my experience that the more things change, the more they stay the same. But sometimes, even when things are as bad as they can get, life can still be very good.

CHAPTER 6

<u>Always Wear Sunscreen</u>

This is why I don't go to the beach. I've only been under the Mayan sun for the better part of an hour and I'm already as red as a boiled New England lobster. It's my own fault really. I am all too aware that my family is genetically predisposed towards keeping in the shade. Despite our mediterranean roots, we just aren't built for the sun. I wonder now if that didn't play a part, no matter how small, in my father and uncle's decision to immigrate from Malta to the US. But given how I currently feel like I've been shrink wrapped into a leotard made out of a colony of ants, I wouldn't be surprised at all if it did.

And yet all my life I have stubbornly refused to put on sunscreen. I didn't even bother packing any for this trip knowing full well my journey would take me south of the equator. Yes, we had to leave in a hurry. But it was a long drive across three states and I had ample opportunity to pick up a tube or two along the way. The truth is that I just don't like the way it feels. It's as simple as that. It's for that same reason that I don't get massages. Any kind of viscous liquid applied on my body makes me want to crawl out of my own skin because of how acutely foreign it feels.

Which once again begs the question of why I ever let Ellie talk me into moving? When most people hear California they immediately think sun and surf and sand. The sunshine state (even though that's Florida). And while that may be accurate to a large extent, it certainly wasn't the default setting in Los Osos. No, the pleasantly mild year-round climate there made for warm winters and cool summers, which suited my needs just fine.

I think it all comes down to the humidity. Dry heat I can handle well enough. But this, the way the air feels here - prickly, surly almost - I don't know if I can ever get used to that. I think I've sweat more in the last 24 hours than I have in my entire life. That's what will be the end of me. Not Chase, or the Cartels, or whatever other new nasty surprise is probably waiting around the corner. The humidity will be what finally does me in. One day I'm going to lay down and simply melt into a puddle like a snowman on a tanning bed.

I hear Ellie and Lauren chatting animatedly as they walk up behind me, but I am unable to turn around because it hurts when I move.

"Did you try the jacuzzi on the roof yet?" My cousin asks my girlfriend. "It's simply to… Oh my. Hello Nick. Doing a little sunbathing are we?"

Lauren is a bit more forthcoming. "Nick! What have you done to yourself?"

"Don't blame me." I retort. "I couldn't sleep so I came out here to watch the sunrise. I was going to go for a swim but there's too much seaweed in the water. Does it really look as bad as it feels?"

"If you feel like a freshly baked ham then yes. Yes it does." Ellie chimes in.

I finally turn around, wincing as my sun-drenched skin stretches across my back like tanned leather. All that discomfort instantly takes a backseat to my laughter when I see my cousin Ellie covered from head to toe in an absurd amount of sunblock.

"Who are you supposed to be, the ghost of Shelley Winters?" I joke.

"Laugh it up, Cuz. Unlike you, I freely acknowledge our family's adversarial relationship with the sun." She snaps back. 'Don't just stand there, Ellie. Give him some of your sunblock." Lauren pleads.

"I don't have any left." Ellie says. "You don't say." I utter sarcastically.

Ellie shoots me one of her withering looks. "Crack wise all you want, Nick. I'm not the one whose going to have to sleep standing up tonight."

She folds her arms across her chest, letting her words sink in.

"I think I may need to go to a hospital." I admit, more to myself than to them.

CHAPTER 7
<u>Man About Town</u>

I begrudgingly allow Lauren and Ellie to hold bags of ice against my shoulders while I hobble to the SUV like I've just been tackled by the entire defensive line of the 1976 Pittsburg Steelers. Miguel, one of the police officers tasked with protecting us, helps me to climb inside. After the ladies clamber in after me, Ellie consults the search engine on the communal mobile phone that has been provided to us courtesy of the Mexican government.

"Llévanos al hospital por favor." She asks the young officer as he gets behind the wheel, the grip of his sidearm peeking out from its holster. He gives her a brisk nod and then starts the car, informing us in impeccable English that there is a clinic near the center of town. I grit my teeth when Lauren drapes a towel over my bare shoulders. This is what I imagine a medieval hair shirt must feel like.

For the first ten minutes of the ride I can focus on little else but the phantom ants nibbling on my back, a thousand tiny pincers piercing my skin with every jostle of the vehicle as it crunches along.

I feel the road suddenly transition from gravel to asphalt, peripherally aware of the scenery gradually changing from dusty skeletal brambles into lush overgrown thickets. At last my scattershot thoughts begin to settle, the wild unresolved landscape outside taming my wandering mind.

I'm ordinarily not very generous when it comes to compliments, even during my teaching days my praise was notoriously hard earned; but to describe the town of Tulum as enchanting would be an understatement of the highest magnitude. And even though my body still feels like it's on fire, and my skin has been threatening to peel off for the last half hour, I can't help but gaze out the backseat window and marvel at where I am.

We drive past a long row of rustic-styled boutique hotels and open air restaurants, their eclectic designs and decor inspired by the vast blue waters and the jungle forests of a simpler time. The distinct aroma of grilled meat from the taquerias wafts in through the air-conditioning vents, filling the car with the mouthwatering tang of cumin and lime.

Even while still within the confines of our vehicle I can already feel the town's allure, it calls out to me, inviting me to leave the relative safety of the SUV and partake in what looks to be a decidedly relaxed ambiance and bohemian atmosphere. My second brain slowly takes over, the cartoon devil on my shoulder telling me that the hospital can wait. My inner excursionist, while definitely slow to awaken, is now on his second cup of Mundo Novo coffee .

"Pull over please. I'd like to get out." I inform Miguel. "You'd like to what now?" Lauren asks me incredulously.

The young officer isn't too keen on the idea either. "I must advise you against doing that, Señor Sanders. We have not cleared it with my superiors.".

I brush off his concerns. "I'm sure it will be fine, Miguel. You seem like a very capable young man.", and then I immediately go to work on appealing to Lauren and Ellie's potential intrepidness, issuing them a challenge of sorts.

"Come on ladies, where's your sense of adventure? How often will we get to experience something like this together? If you ask me the best place to be is right here. The best time to be is right now. So who's with me?"

"Sure, why not?" Ellie shrugs. "Count me in, Cuz. This place looks like a hoot. And I need to pick up some more sunblock…"

With Ellie on board, Lauren warms to the prospect of some sightseeing. "Well, when you put it that way. This place *is* awfully pretty…"

We wander the cobblestone streets, riding the wave of good natured locals patiently co-existing alongside flamboyantly dressed day-trippers from every corner of the globe, gawking at the sights like the tourists that we all are. I grab a map of the town from a magazine rack in front of a specialty liquor store, intrigued by the hundreds of bottles of tequila and mezcal that line its walls in every conceivable shape and size. But Lauren and Ellie are more interested in the souvenir shops that are displaying their wares right on the crowded sidewalks, inspecting the hodgepodge of colorful bracelets and intricately beaded necklaces, the 10-gallon sombreros and the Spaghetti Western ponchos, the hand woven straw baskets and the whimsical Mexican wrestling masks. I read in one of the guide books at the villa that Tulum can be something of a tourists trap, but I know for a fact that there are much less desirable places to be trapped in.

I notice a beautiful young Latina woman with long raven hair stealing glances at me from across the street. She has an air of mystery about her, with her secrets hidden behind dark sunglasses. Although she pretends not to be, I am fairly certain that she is watching me. To what end I cannot be sure. I briefly entertain the notion that she might find me attractive, but I banish that thought as fast as it comes. She looks like trouble with a capital T, and gladly, I am already spoken for.

As if on cue, Lauren tugs on my fingers and hands me a T-shirt shirt she has just purchased. "Here, I got this for you. See if it fits."

I hold the shirt out wide in front of me, and I smile at her thoughtfulness. It says 'I Love Tulum'. This is accurate. Because while it has not occurred to me until this very moment, I have been walking around bare chested this whole time, the charms of Tulum having effectively dulled my sunburn.

"Shall we go? Ellie wants to find a convenience store where she can buy her sunblock. You should seriously think about getting some yourself… " Lauren says as she helps me wiggle into my new shirt, my pink skin still tender.

"And then we can get some brunch. I'm starving. Everything smells like food here." Ellie adds, examining her haul of souvenir goodies.

"Lead the way." I say, looking back and seeing that the young woman is gone, having vanished just as mysteriously as she appeared.

CHAPTER 8
The Señorita Next Door

Midnight has long come and gone, but I am still far too invigorated from my excursion into town to even entertain the thought of sleep. So I do what I always do when things start to pile up inside my head. I go for a late night stroll. Today I was acutely aware of my otherness, but here, under a canopy of stars, I decide that's a good thing. I am an outlier, a disruptor, a wrench thrown into the machinations of powerful men. Which in turn also makes me a powerful man.

I walk along the beach, the cool sand under my bare feet, a tender breeze tussling my hair. I determine that I have allowed life to slip through my fingers for long enough. The gentle ebb and flow of the tide upon the shore succinctly embodies my newfound tranquility, allowing my thoughts to coalesce - From now on my plans will be fluid. I no longer have anything I ever asked and hoped for in my early years, but through a serpentine series of events new dreams and desires have revealed themselves. My carefully laid out life of button-down blue work shirts has been replaced by exotically patterned Tommy Bahama's and open-toed sandals. A sufficient life just doesn't suit me any longer, and I am excited by the knowledge that I do not know what will. It's as Tennyson wrote in his poem

Ulysses, "To strive, to seek, to find, and not to yield." So, I walk slowly and I wait for the cosmos to aim me.

I don't wait but more than a minute before I hear a series of loud bangs go off in the still night. Gun shots? It can't be… What are the odds that this is happening again? I suppose they are higher than average when it comes to me. I know the sound of gunshots all too well. But tonight I'm not sure what I just heard. Perhaps the possibility that I may stumble upon yet another staged suicide in so short a time is playing havoc with my aptitude for aural discrimination. Either way, the chills don't shake me the way they had the first time. When you find out that your chin isn't made of glass you don't disregard a sound that signals death, you walk toward it.

A group of rowdy young men chattering with thick English accents stumble past me. I was a tenured professor at a prestigious American university, I know how to spot drunk college kids when I see them. One of them sees me staring and lights something in his hand, tossing it at my feet.

I stupidly bend down to get a better look, the wick almost completely singed away before I realize what it is. I scramble toward the ocean as fast as my doddering knees will allow, specks of light sparking off behind me as the darkness ignites with a crackle. I'm not fond of many of things, firecrackers being close to the top of that list. By the time I get back up to my feet the group has disappeared down the beach, boisterous laughter fading away as the night resets to its natural state.

"Mexico is a haven for the saint and the sinner alike." A velvety voice declares with a lyrical cadence.

I see a woman standing on the shore like the specter of some Mayan princess, the waves lapping at her bare feet, the glow of the moonlight casting a gentle aura over her bronzed skin. I recognize her immediately. It's the mysterious woman from town.

"And which are you? Sinner or Saint?" I ask as I oafishly brush away the sand from my thighs.

"That depends on who you ask." She replies playfully, her coy smile a gash upon my composure.

I step forward clumsily with my hand outstretched, only too eager to introduce myself. "I'm Nicholas. Nick. Nick Sanders. *Professor* Sanders if we're being particular." I boast.

"I am always particular." She answers as she shakes my hand, her lithe fingers grazing my palm. "I am Irina. I have noticed you, Nick. I believe that we are neighbors."

And there's my answer for why she was staring at me earlier, she recognized me from the beach. I sure hope that it wasn't while I was blistering in the sun, because that would be truly embarrassing.

"So you are a professor. I find this very interesting." She tells me as she ties her hair back into a ponytail. "What subject of life are you a professor of?"

"English." I blurt out, suddenly aware of how pedestrian it sounds out loud. "But I'm retired now."

"You have retired from teaching people how to speak in English?" She asks, puzzled.

"Well no… I taught my students about literary works. Literary movements. Authors. Poets. All aspects of the English language really." I clarify. It's a tailored reply I always carry handy in my back pocket. She's not the first person to misunderstand what I did for a living.

"Ah. I think I understand. 'To Thine Own self be true' correct?" She asks in her captivating accent, endearingly placing an emphasize on all the wrong syllables.

"Correct!" I exclaim, tickled pink by her quoting of Hamlet. "I see you are familiar with The Bard."

"Is not everyone able to quote Shakespeare where you are from?" Irina quips, allowing her dress to fall to the sand as she steps into the moonlight in her swimsuit. "Won't you join me for a swim, Professor Nick?"

"No, thank you." I demure, thrown for a loop by her nonchalance. "This is how the movie Jaws started. Have you ever seen that film? It's quite good." I ramble on, clutching at every stray thought within reach to distract me from the fact that there is a beautiful woman not named Lauren asking me to join her for a dip in the Gulf of Mexico. To paraphrase a treasured American author 'It's no wonder that truth is stranger than fiction, fiction has to make sense.'

"The only sharks you must worry about are the kind that walk on two feet." Irina warns and breaks into a run, striding against the waves before diving headlong in the surf.

I don't realize I'm holding my breath while I wait for her to break the surface. But after a few minutes panic begins to tickle my amygdala. No one can go this long without air unless they are a seasoned free diver. Where could she be? Did she swim out past the breakers? Did she resurface further down the beach just to rattle me; a cruel joke in retaliation for refusing to join her in the water? I stare out into the vast obsidian ocean, my eyes darting between every shape and shadow I can make out in the darkness. I am about to pass out from the stress when I feel a tap on my shoulder; wet and cold like a recently used ice pick. I spin around on my heels to find Irina behind me, laughing at my unabashed relief to discover that she hasn't drowned after all.

"Aloe." She says when she finally catches her breath. "Hello yourself, young lady!" I snap back, my annoyance suddenly bordering on full fledged anger.

"No. Not hello. *Aloe*." She corrects me, enunciating her words for the confused English professor. "To soothe your skin. There is a plant that grows in my garden. Come by tomorrow and I will give you some."

"Uh, okay. Maybe." Are the only words I manage to eke out, astonished by her flagrant indifference to the harrowing emotional journey she has just taken me on.

"Good night, Professor Nick. Hasta mañana." Irina says matter-of-factly, oblivious to the bullseye I have mentally affixed to her back as she saunters away.

I find myself alone once again, forced to re-evaluate my earlier catharsis, my fervent resolutions under threat of being swept away like so much confetti the day after a New Year's Eve celebration.

CHAPTER 9
Welcomed Into The Shadows With Open Arms

My eyes flutter open and I see Marco sitting at the foot of my bed like a boogeyman in the darkness, entirely too comfortable in the twilight shadows. Everybody dreams when they sleep, it's a scientific fact, but most times we forget what we were dreaming about just as soon as we wake up. My dreams have not been very reassuring as of late, so I am grateful that this is one of those times. Especially since my waking life has now begun to resemble a nightmare.

Marco presses a finger against his lips and points to the sliding doors leading out on to the balcony. I nod, looking over at Lauren to make sure she is still sound asleep before I follow after him.

We watch the sunrise without saying a word to each other. I'm not much in the mood to talk anyway. My skin itches, the pink tenderness having settled into an ashen brown while I slept, a husk begging to be peeled. Although my joints ache and hum from a lack of any proper rest, Marco's sudden presence here has unnerved me so much that I'm as jittery as an insomniac in a mattress emporium.

"Late night, Nick?" He finally asks, his face betraying little emotion.

"What are you doing here, Marco? Could this not have waited?" I ask, my temper getting the better of me. I immediately regret snapping at him. I must not forget that this man is one of only a handful of people I can call friend here, and it's by his good graces that me and my loved ones are safe. But if my flare up bothers him i any way, he hides it well.

"I'm afraid not, compadre. A Gulfstream G650 landed at a private airstrip in Veracruz late last night. A man matching Chase Slate's description was seen deplaning. But by the time my people arrived at the airfield I'm afraid it was already too late…" He says almost apologetically.

So Chase is now in Mexico. Does he know that I'm here? Or is he merely taking refuge within the criminal underworld of the cartels? I suppose only time will tell. We are connected now he and I, perhaps destined for some kind of final showdown. And if or when that time comes, I will be ready.

"So what do we do now?" I ask, nervously scratching at a patch of dry skin.

"Now you come with me. There are some people who would very much like to meet you." He says enigmatically.

"What about Lauren and Ellie?" I ask, looking past Marco into the room.

"They will be safe while we are away." He assure me. "As you mentioned yesterday, Miguel is a capable young man. And he is not alone."

How does he know about that I wonder… Is the SUV bugged, or did Miguel simply report back to his superiors like a dutiful police officer would?

"We have eyes and ears everywhere, compadre." He shares as if reading my mind. "Get dressed. Do it quietly. We must go now. Crime does not sleep, depriving us of that luxury as well." My latest antagonist, the sun, has yet emerge in all its full sweltering magnificence as we drive away from the villa. I feel guilty leaving the way that I am, but hopefully the note I left on the bedside table will explain things some. Lauren and Ellie won't be happy, but maybe my hastily scribbled words of '*Off to save the world. Be back soonest.*' will dull their anger a little bit. I highly doubt that my attempt at humor will , but a man can dream can't he?

The next hour goes by in a haze of mariachi music assaulting me from the radio, our SUV speeding down a highway that skirts the blue water edges of the peninsula, a panorama of heavily forested lowlands abruptly ending in either jagged cliffs or powder white beaches.

We eventually pull up in front of a deserted hotel on the brink of nowhere, the ten story centerpiece of a sprawling seaside resort still under heavy construction. It does not take much to imagine that this place, once finished, will play host to a plethora of wide-eyed gringos just like me.

As soon as I hop out of the vehicle I am swarmed by soldiers in tactical gear, thoroughly poking and prodding at every nook and cranny of my body, proceeding to turning my duffle bag inside out and scrutinize its contents - Mostly old newspaper clippings I liberated from the Los Osos library.

Once the soldiers are satisfied that I'm just a harmless old man without any dangerous weapons to speak of beyond my quick wit and an encyclopedic knowledge of Frank Sinatra's discography, they allow me through.

A barrel-chested Mexican gentleman with thick landscaped eyebrows walks out of the hotel doors in full military regalia, introducing himself while still walking toward me with an outstretched hand.

"Buenos días, Señor Sanders. I apologize for the thoroughness of my men. One cannot be sure about the company they keep during these *peligroso* times. I am *General* Felix Ignacio de Castillo. Head of the *Secretaría de la Defensa Nacional*. Marco's boss."

I nod as I shake his hand, acting like his rank means something to me. And I suppose it should, the way his men look upon him with such deference. I've never served in the military myself, and the closest I've ever been to actual warfare has been while watching a Ken Burns documentary, but even an avowed civilian such as myself is able to comprehend that this is an important man.

"If you will come this way please. We have a proposition for you." The General says vaguely.

I turn to Marco. "Who's we?" I ask, hoping for just a sliver of clarity.

"Welcome to the shadows, compadre. There is now turning back now." He says slyly, his lopsided grin pregnant with enough significance it fills my empty stomach with unease. If I walk away from all this intrigue and double talk with just an ulcer it will be a bonafide Lady of Guadalupe miracle…

CHAPTER 10

Baiting the Hook

"So basically what you all are saying is you want to use me as bait…" I ask a room full of important looking men that are all staring at me like a parliament of owls from behind an unnecessarily large banquet table, resting on all their unspoken laurels as they hungrily eye me from their perches like the mouse that I have somehow become.

The room I'm in is already intimidating enough; four square walls lined with the portraits of stern-faced men I can only assume are the former heads of this clandestine group. Did they fly these portraits in and hang them up especially for me? Or are they at every cloak-and-dagger assembly of a shadow council? Regardless of the answers, whatever they are selling me, I fear I may have no choice but to buy.

"Bait is such a strong word. Incentive is more applicable perhaps?" General Castillo clarifies in an effort to assuage my mounting concerns, which you don't need to be a spy-master to notice.

"Bait. Incentive. Those are both synonyms to me right now." I counter with an extra helping of snark, my false bravado a hastily constructed house of cards - Impressive at first glance yet ultimately hollow. Much like the building we are in.

"I told you he would not be up for the task, Don Castillo. We should explore other avenues." Squawks the man seated next to the General, a nebbish man in his 40s with an unabashed disdain for me. "Americans only wish to involve themselves in affairs they may benefit from. It has been their way since their so called manifest destiny."

"Now hold on a minute, Señor whoever-you-are. I never said I wasn't up to the task. I just think we should clarify what we're all talking about here. You people brought me to your country with an idea to use me as a lure to tempt Chase Slate out into open. Is that not the case?"

"I apologize for my assistant's outburst. He makes travels to your country often on my behalf. Needless to say, he is not a, cómo se dice? He is not a fan." The General explains.

"Well you can tell your assistant…" I begin crisply before my newfound nemesis cuts me off.

"You may address me as Lucas Garza, señor. I am the General's left hand, the hand that holds the knife. I am not some nameless Peruvian immigrant for you to talk at." He pipes in haughtily, the spittle probably aimed at my face dribbling down his lower lip.

"Fine then. I'm sorry, Luke. But I could care less what you think about us Americans. Bottom line is that it's my butt on the line here, not yours." I remind him, taking care to keep my voice at a reasonable decibel.

"Caballeros, I fear this discussion has strayed from its intentions. I would ask you both to restrain yourselves. There are more important things at stake than wounded pride." The General chastises. "Señor Sanders. Marco has told us that after only a few days spent in an *American* library you were able to uncover Chase Slate's entire California operation. Is this correct?"

"I guess. I mean, I had help. And I got beaten up a lot. But in a nutshell, sure." I answer modestly, which is actually closer to the truth than I would like to admit.

The General stands, pressing his palms flat on the table. "Yes, should you decide to help us, it will come at great personal risk to yourself. But despite Señor Garza's low opinion of you and your country, have not you Americans risked much less for much more?

I know what this crafty man is doing. He thinks he is stoking some esoterically ingrained sense of duty in me that is fundamentally inherent in every citizen of the United States of America. It's not *not* working.

"Chase Slate's operation spans the entire globe, from the Golden Triangle of Southeast Asia to the unregulated ports of Eastern Europe. And there does all this poison find a home? On my country's shores. We must cut the head off the snake. Can you help us, señor? The General beseeches me.

"Did you just mention the Golden Triangle? That's where all the speed is from right?" I ask excitedly, dumping the contents of my duffle bag onto the table.

"One of the things I uncovered while I was pouring through all the Los Osos archives was this editorial by my friend Maddy from 10 years ago." I continue. "It says an SUV was pulled over and the driver arrested after a sizable amount of methamphetamine was discovered inside."

"Why should we care about this?" Garza asks snappishly.

"Because the SUV was registered to one Chase Slate!" I announce, holding up the newspaper clipping to drive home my point. But despite my exuberance, my revelation met with blank faces.

"And what does that matter?" The newest addition to my growing rogues gallery asks.

"The driver died in his cell. Under suspicious circumstances." I gush, eager to shut him up.

"Señor Sanders, while I applaud your tenaciousness. Chase Slate has already been arrested in your country on much more serious crimes." The General reminds me.

"Oh. Right." Is all I can say, kicking myself for my feeble attempt at avoiding to enlarge the target that has already been painted on my back.

"I understand your reasons for not wanting to help us. You have done enough. This is no longer your concern. Please enjoy the villa in Tulum. You and your companions may stay as long as you desire." The General says, turning away from me to consults the other members gathered around the table.

I walk out of the hotel and turn to Marco. "I'm still going to be the bait aren't I?" I ask, already knowing the answer.

"You're still going to be the bait." Marco answers bluntly.

"Welcome to the bigger world."

CHAPTER 11

When Trust Withers, Uncertainty Blooms

J.R.R. Tolkien once wrote that 'not all who wander are lost'. He wasn't actually talking about physically being lost of course, but instead, he was emphasizing a state of mind. The passage is a reminder that no matter how difficult or meandering the journey may be, if taken with conviction, all roads eventually lead you to your destination. I however, have been wandering, and I am most certainly lost. My latest excursion has taken me far beyond my threshold for adventure, and back into the gutters of my inner psyche. It's an unpleasant place where all I understand is fear. From a locational standpoint, I know exactly where I am. I'm back at the villa, a cold Modelo sweating in my hand, listening to Ellie and Lauren give me an earful of their disapproval. But while I may be physically present, my mind is everywhere and nowhere all at once, and their concern-driven castigations flow over me like a river over mossy rock.

"No two ways about it, Cuz. I want to go home. I miss my girlfriend. I miss my house. I miss my life." I hear Ellie declare angrily as soon as I tune back in, although I still find it hard to take her too seriously when she's wearing a day's worth of sunblock on her face alone.

Lauren unexpectedly comes to my defense. "But that would be like jumping out of the frying pan and into the fire, wouldn't it? I agree that Nick shouldn't have left like he did, but let's not make any hasty decisions. I mean, surely we're safer here than back there."

"Actually, going back to Los Osos might be the best thing for us to do right now." I admit.

"What are you talking about, Nick? You were the one that insisted we come all the way out here where we would be safe." Lauren asks, her face just as puzzled as Ellie's.

"They think Chase is here in Mexico." I confess, unable to bring my eyes up to meet theirs.

"Way to bury the lead, Nicholas!" Ellie sputters and my heart sinks a little bit. She only calls me Nicholas when she's especially disappointed in me.

"Do they *think* or do they *know*?" Lauren tries to clarify, her face taking on an anemic pallor.

"I think they know. Someone that looks like him flew in last night." I explain, conveniently leaving out the part where a covert group of Mexican spooks want to use us as bait. The boat has already been well and thoroughly rocked, so why capsize it?

"Everyone be quiet. Someone's coming." Lauren cautions, instantly plastering a smile on her face, the effortless shift from gamma-eyed Bill Bixby to Martha Stewart quite disconcerting. "Is it Chase?" I squeak, yet ready to use my beer bottle as a weapon should the need arise.

"Not unless his master plan involves him getting extensive plastic surgery to look like Sophia Loren…" Ellie mutters acerbically, her SPF-100 lathered eyebrows still furrowed from my revelation.

Baffled by her statement, I quickly look over my shoulder to see Irina in a bikini that leaves little to the imagination walking up the pathway toward us.

"Buenas tardes, Nick!" She greets me enthusiastically, waving with one hand while carrying a fishnet tote bag filled with serrated edged leaves in the other.

I feel Lauren's gaze upon me, tickling the back of my neck like a Velociraptor talon. "Nick... Who is that gorgeous woman and why does she know your name?"

"I met her on the beach last night, honey. She's our neighbor." I offer up nonchalantly, an effort to placate my girlfriend before she can pull me back into the villa by the ear. "Hi, Irina. What are you doing here?" I ask, stowing away any indication that I am pleased to see her.

"You did not come to visit me this morning to soothe your sunburn. If the mountain will not come to me, then I must come to the mountain, yes?" She answers, flashing me a smile that would send every Greek man across the Aegean to lay siege to the fabled walls of Troy itself.

Lauren bristles like a sea urchin as Irina strolls up to the patio, her bronzed skin sparkling under the punishing afternoon sun as if she were dusted in diamond shavings.

"Here is the aloe I promised you." She says, slapping a handful of moist leaves on my lap with an audible crunch that just about shatters my fragile composure.

Irina turns to Lauren and Ellie, who at this point have eschewed any modicum of decorum.

"I'm Lauren. Nick's *girlfriend*." She blurts out territorially.

"That's *quite* the swimsuit you have on."

"Thank you, Lauren. Nick's girlfriend. It covers up what it needs to. I am Irina. I stay in the villa down the beach." Irina responds, unfazed by the unabashed vitriol in Lauren's voice.

"Hi. I'm Ellie. I like your swimsuit too." My cousin gushes, unable or unwilling to take her eyes off the woman's glistening cleavage as she juts her hand forward.

"Hello, Ellie. It is a pleasure to meet you both. If it is not too much trouble, may I please use your outdoor shower? I fear I shall end up like our dear friend Nick here if I do not wash this salt off of my body." Irina asks with an affected pout.

Lauren starts to protest but Ellie heads her off at the pass. "It's no trouble at all. That's what it's there for right? I can walk you over if you like…" She offers eagerly.

"Thank you, Ellie. But I think I can manage to find my way from here." She declines tactfully, "But when I return, perhaps we should open the bottle of tequila in my bag and drink to new friendships, yes?" Her breezy self-assured delivery assuring Ellie's goo goo-eyed acquiescence.

We all watch her shower, trying our best not to ogle as the stream of water from the shower-head cascades down her body in ripples, but for reasons unique to each of us we cannot look away.

Lauren elbows me in my side. "You better believe we're gonna talk about this once Miss Hawaiian Tropic is gone. And you, Ellie. You have a girlfriend back home." She chastises.

"She's a very understanding woman." Ellie contends, "We have a look but don't touch policy."

A rapid flutter of muted pops suddenly fills the air, just loud enough for me to tear my attention away from Irina and over to the villa. I watch in horror as Miguel crashes through the sliding glass doors, landing on his back with a wet slap on the edge of the swimming pool, the blood oozing from his gaping wounds turning the water red. It seems I must amend my earlier statement, I recognize the song of gunshots only when they matter…

I react wholly on instinct, grabbing both Lauren and Ellie by the arm and pulling them behind the safety of the long bar, the bottles of liquor on the shelves above us exploding in a hail of glass and alcohol. Irina appears at our side, reaching into her bag and pulling out a Colt M1911 semi-automatic pistol with a customized rattlesnake-skin grip. I'm a writer, I notice these things.

She grabs me by the collar of my shirt and yanks me close, yelling at me over the hail of suppressed machine gunfire. "Do what I say if you want to live!"

"Who are you?" I shout, my eyes so wide you can chart the spider-web of broken blood vessels all the way down into the deepest recesses of my terrified soul.

"I work for Mexico. I work for Marco." She answers before she stands to return fire.

"Is Irina even your name?" I ask her when she crouches back down to reload.

"Why does this matter right now, cabrón?" She snaps, her priorities obviously elsewhere.

"Nick, I think there are more pressing issues than her name right now!" Lauren screams, her hair flecked with broken glass. She is right of course, the battlefield is no place for trivial questions. And make no mistake, our villa has undoubtedly become a battlefield. Yet I refuse to let it go.

"Is Irina your real name?" I ask again as the alluring woman I met on the beach just the night before ducks back down, smoke visibly wafting from the barrel of her gun.

"You're crazy, gringo… Has anyone ever told you that?" She asks, something bordering on respect flickering in her eyes.

"All the time." I answer, somehow calmer in all this chaos for the look she has just given me.

"My name is Karina. Are you happy now? Now do as I say. When I return fire you and your friends must run and not look back." She instructs me, taking a deep breath to steady herself. I have no idea whether I can trust her or not, for all I know she could be ushering us right into Chase's waiting arms, but the halo of indiscriminate gunfire leaves me with no choice. I grab Lauren and Ellie by the wrist and place their hands on either side of my shoulders.

"Whatever happens, don't lose me." I tell them, realizing I sound like a supporting character in a Charles Bronson movie. Irina grits her teeth and then stands, the deafening recoil from her gun almost drowning out her desperate pleas for me to "Run!"

"I am the outlier!" I shriek as we run towards the beach. Intended to be my war cry, it falls woefully short as Lauren and Ellie grip my shoulders so tightly that the end of my sentence is stifled by my own grunts of pain, their fingers peeling off the burnt skin on my back wholesale.

I am Job, instructed not to look back while my whole world crumbles behind me. But like Job I look back anyway, watching my whole world crumble behind me.

CHAPTER 12
Into the Abyss

The villa transforms into a chaotic tableau of violence and destruction. Bullets rip through the air, shattering windows, splintering furniture, and leaving trails of devastation in their wake. The once idyllic retreat has become a battleground, and the safety I had sought has been shattered like glass.

As we sprint towards the beach, fear propels us forward, our hearts pounding with adrenaline. The sound of gunshots echoes in my ears, drowning out all other noise. I can feel the heat of the bullets whizzing past, narrowly missing their mark. It's a dance with death, and we're desperate to stay one step ahead.

Irina, or rather Karina, leads the way, her gun held firmly in her hands, her eyes focused and determined. She moves with a grace and precision that belies her stunning appearance. There is a coldness in her gaze, a steely resolve that makes me question her true motives. But in this moment, she is our best chance at survival.

We reach the edge of the beach, the sand cool beneath our feet. The waves crash against the shore, a stark contrast to the chaos behind us. Karina motions for us to keep running, her voice lost in the symphony of gunfire. We follow her lead, our strides fueled by desperation and the will to live.

As we race along the shoreline, I steal a glance over my shoulder. The villa is engulfed in flames, the fire licking at the walls, consuming everything in its path. It's a stark reminder of the danger we've left behind, the peril that continues to chase us.

The sound of a motor roars in the distance, growing louder with each passing moment. I turn my gaze towards the sea and see a speedboat approaching, cutting through the water with swift precision. Karina must have arranged for an escape route—a lifeline amidst the chaos.

We reach the water's edge, our lungs burning, our bodies pushed to their limits. Karina signals for us to get into the boat, her voice finally audible above the cacophony.

"Get in! We don't have much time!" she shouts, her eyes scanning the shoreline for any signs of pursuit.

I help Lauren and Ellie into the boat, their hands trembling with fear and exhaustion. Once they're safely aboard, I turn to Karina, unsure of what lies ahead.

"What about you?" I ask, my voice strained.

"I'll cover your escape. Go, now!" she replies, her gaze unwavering.

Reluctantly, I step into the boat, the engine rumbling beneath me. The boat starts to move, slowly at first, and then with increasing speed. I watch as Karina stays behind, her gun raised, a lone figure against the backdrop of chaos.

As the boat carries us away from the shore, I can't help but feel a pang of guilt for leaving Karina behind. She had saved us, guided us to safety, and now she remains in the line of fire. I wonder if she will make it out alive, if she was truly on our side or if she had her own agenda.

The questions swirl in my mind, but they are drowned out by the sound of the boat's engine and the crashing waves. We sail into the unknown, leaving the nightmare behind but carrying its weight with us.

In the confines of the boat, I turn to Lauren and Ellie, their faces etched with exhaustion and fear. We lock eyes, silent acknowledgment passing between us. We have survived, but the battle is far from over. The shadows of uncertainty loom before us, and we must find the strength to navigate through the darkness.

As the boat glides further into the horizon, I can't help but wonder what awaits us on the other side. The road ahead is treacherous, and the path to safety is laden with obstacles. But we will endure. We will fight. For in the face of adversity, there is a flicker of hope—a glimmer that refuses to be extinguished.

And so, we sail on, our fates intertwined, searching for answers amidst the chaos, and hoping that someday we will find our way back to the light.

CHAPTER 13

Shattered Loyalties

The boat glides through the open sea, the rhythmic rocking motion providing a momentary respite from the turmoil we left behind. The adrenaline begins to subside, replaced by a bone-deep weariness that weighs heavy on our shoulders. The events at the villa replay in my mind, each detail etched into my memory like scars.

Lauren and Ellie huddle together, seeking comfort in each other's presence. Their eyes reflect a mix of relief and trepidation, the trauma of our escape etched on their faces. We share a bond forged in the crucible of danger, but there are still unanswered questions lingering in the air.

I turn my gaze towards the receding shoreline, the flames of the villa fading into the distance. Karina's sacrifice hangs heavy in my thoughts. Was she merely a pawn in a larger game, or did she genuinely intend to help us? The uncertainty gnaws at me, tugging at the fraying edges of trust.

As the boat cuts through the waves, a sense of isolation settles over us. We are adrift in more ways than one—adrift in the vast expanse of the sea, and adrift in a world where our allies and enemies blur together in a haze of uncertainty. We have no choice but to push forward, to seek answers and safety in equal measure.

Hours pass, marked by the setting sun and the gradual transition from daylight to twilight. The boat's engine hums steadily, a constant reminder of our progress. We've traveled a considerable distance, but the weight of our situation hasn't lifted.

A sudden crackle of static breaks the silence, followed by a voice over the boat's radio. It's a voice I don't recognize, distorted by interference, but the urgency in its tone is unmistakable.

"Attention! This is Captain Ramirez of the Coast Guard. We have received reports of gunfire and an explosion at Villa Azul. Please identify yourselves and state your situation."

Relief washes over me as I realize that help may be within reach. I reach for the radio, my voice trembling with a mix of exhaustion and hope.

"This is Alex. We were caught in the violence at Villa Azul. We managed to escape, but we're still in danger. Please, we need assistance."

There's a pause on the other end of the line, and then Captain Ramirez responds.

"Alex, we have your location. Stay put. We're sending a rescue team to your coordinates. Help is on the way."

A surge of gratitude fills me, mingled with a renewed sense of hope. We're not alone in this fight. The Coast Guard knows of our predicament and is coming to our aid. For the first time in what feels like an eternity, the weight on my shoulders eases slightly.

As we wait for the rescue team, conversation fills the air, punctuated by moments of uneasy silence. Lauren breaks the stillness.

"What do you think happened back there, Alex? Was Karina really on our side?"

Her words echo the doubts that have plagued my thoughts since our escape. I pause, searching for an answer that remains elusive.

"I don't know, Lauren. It's hard to say. But for now, we have to focus on getting to safety. Once we're out of this mess, we can try to make sense of everything."

Lauren nods, her expression a mix of understanding and lingering suspicion. We're all grappling with the same questions, the same shattered loyalties. But we must press on, for our own sake and for the truth that awaits us.

Time stretches on, the minutes feeling like hours, until the distant hum of an approaching vessel breaks the stillness. The rescue team has arrived, their boat slicing through the water with purpose. Relief floods through me as we see their familiar uniforms and the outstretched hands ready to pull us to safety.

We transfer to the Coast Guard boat, stepping onto the deck with a mixture of weariness and gratitude. The crew tends to our needs, offering blankets and warm drinks to ease the chill that has settled in our bones. We're no longer alone in this fight, and that knowledge provides solace.

As the Coast Guard boat steers us towards the nearest port, I steal one last glance at the receding horizon. The villa, the chaos, and the unanswered questions remain behind, obscured by the vastness of the sea. But we carry their weight with us, a reminder of the trials we've faced and the truths we seek.

The journey is far from over, but as the lights of the port come into view, a flicker of hope ignites within us. We will find our way through the darkness, shattered loyalties and all. For in the crucible of adversity, strength is born, and the truth will ultimately unveil itself, guiding us towards the light we so desperately seek.

CHAPTER 14
Unraveling Threads

The port comes into view, its bustling activity a stark contrast to the desolation we left behind. The Coast Guard boat docks, and we step onto solid ground once again, our legs wobbly from the hours spent at sea. The rescue team guides us towards a waiting ambulance, their faces a mix of concern and professionalism.

As we settle into the back of the ambulance, the doors close behind us, shutting out the noise of the outside world. The vehicle lurches forward, and the steady hum of the engine lulls us into a state of exhaustion-induced calm.

Inside, the air carries a sterile scent, a stark reminder of the medical environment surrounding us. It's a stark contrast to the chaos we've experienced, a symbol of safety and care. The paramedic tends to our minor injuries, their practiced hands providing comfort in their touch.

Lauren breaks the silence, her voice filled with a mix of gratitude and lingering uncertainty.

"I can't believe we made it out alive," she says, her voice barely above a whisper.

Ellie nods, her eyes reflecting a blend of relief and lingering trauma.

"We owe our lives to the Coast Guard and their quick response. I'll never forget their courage and dedication," she adds.

I chime in, my voice carrying a note of determination.

"But we can't forget the questions that remain unanswered. We need to find out the truth, about Karina and what really happened at Villa Azul. We owe it to ourselves and to those who didn't make it."

Lauren and Ellie exchange glances, their resolve mirrored in their eyes. We're united in our quest for answers, our shared experience forging an unbreakable bond. The ambulance's motion matches the rhythm of our determination, propelling us forward.

The vehicle comes to a stop, and the doors swing open, revealing the entrance to a small coastal hospital. We step out, the cool evening air washing over us, a soothing balm for our weary souls. Inside, the hospital staff tends to our needs, offering warm blankets and reassurance.

As we wait for further examination, a detective enters the room, her eyes sharp and attentive. She introduces herself as Detective Rodriguez and explains that she has been assigned to investigate the events at Villa Azul. Her presence brings a glimmer of hope, a renewed sense that answers may be within reach.

Detective Rodriguez takes a seat and begins to ask us questions, piecing together the fragments of our ordeal. We recount our harrowing escape, the violence that unfolded, and our encounter with Karina. The detective listens intently, her notebook capturing the details that may hold the key to unraveling the truth.

After hours of questioning, Detective Rodriguez thanks us for our cooperation and assures us that she will do everything in her power to uncover the truth. We exchange contact information, a lifeline that may connect us to the answers we seek.

Days turn into weeks as we wait for news from the detective. The hospital releases us with clean bills of health, and we find temporary refuge in a nearby coastal town. The sea breeze offers solace, its rhythmic waves a reminder of the ever-present ebb and flow of life.

One evening, as the sun dips below the horizon, a message arrives—a call from Detective Rodriguez. She informs us that her investigation has led to significant discoveries. Karina, whose real name is Irina, has a complex history of involvement with criminal organizations. Her true allegiance remains unclear, but evidence suggests that she had been operating under the guise of Karina to infiltrate Villa Azul.

The revelations hit us like a tidal wave, shattering the remnants of trust we had left. We had been deceived, caught in a web spun by a woman with her own agenda. The questions that had haunted us find some semblance of an answer, but it's a bitter truth to swallow.

Detective Rodriguez promises to continue her investigation, to dig deeper into the tangled web of lies and deceit. We find solace in her determination, in the knowledge that someone is fighting for the truth.

As we navigate the aftermath of the chaos, we realize that our journey is far from over. The road to justice and closure stretches out before us, a labyrinth of secrets waiting to be unraveled. The threads of our lives remain entangled, bound by the shared experience that forever changed us.

Armed with newfound determination, we set out to find our own answers, to confront the shadows that linger in the corners of our minds. We will peel back the layers of deception, determined to expose the truth and reclaim our lives from the clutches of darkness.

Together, we embark on a new chapter, propelled by the strength forged through adversity, and fueled by the unwavering belief that the light will prevail, even in the darkest of nights.

CHAPTER 15
<u>War Ensemble</u>

All the police officers and soldiers are standing behind velvet ropes lined up along the hotel lobby, applauding my now undeniable courage as soon as I walk in. I strut across the red carpet they have rolled out for me, past all the men jostling to be the first one to raise my hand up in the air triumphantly... Which was the welcome I was hoping against hope to receive in my head.

The reality is far more sobering - A few terse nods from mostly untested young warriors as money discretely changes hands. And from the minuscule amounts I see in play I have to assume that not a single one of them was ever really betting on me to begin with. Which is demoralizing to be sure, but nowhere near as daunting as waiting for the elevator to arrive and take me back up to join the self-styled overlords of this beautiful country in their gallery of citrus-sour faces.

The officer who rides up in the elevator with Marco and I is a stone-faced colossus, the brim of his service cap nearly blocking the orbital camera affixed to the wall that is watching our every move.

I consider a few ways that I might lighten the mood in here but dismiss them all almost immediately, fighting back my reflexive need to fill uncomfortable silences with humor or Snapple cap fun facts, determined to at least *seem* at ease with my brash choices in the eyes of the professional liars club.

But a loud ding announces that we have arrived at the very top of the tower, and as the doors slowly slide open I am quickly reduced to the sum of all my fears, instantly hit with the realization that I am the foolish gringo lamb who has demanded to be led to its own slaughter.

We are greeted by a nebbish functionary who promptly introduces himself as Ricardo, my new assistant. Which is already a marked improvement from the way I've been treated by these people up until now. Yet what it takes to shore up some much-needed resolve inside me is the sight of a very angry-looking Lucas Garza sitting just outside the war room like a little boy on a time out.

I can't help but jut my chin out at him as I am ushered through the double-wide mahogany doors, and into the waiting embrace of moral grayness from whence there is sure to be no return.

As the doors are slammed shut and bolted behind me, I immediately notice that the large banquet table has been converted into a shockingly detailed physical representation of targets and objectives, all dedicated to the utter dismantlement of Chase's entire west coast operation. As a man reliant on structure and beholden to fastidiousness, I have no choice but to be completely impressed.

"Welcome, Doctor Saunders. I expect this meets your high standards?" The General asks, the question delivered with such definitiveness so as to render any answer I give inconsequential.

"I must confess, General. This is not… not what what I was expecting…" I reluctantly admit, still in awe at the meticulousness and totality with which his plan of action has been assembled.

"Did you truly think us so inept and undeserving of your regard?" The General chuckles in a rare showing of emotion. "We have been doing this a long time, Doctor. Chase Slate is not the first person whose activities have threatened my country, nor am I under any disillusions that he will be the last." He scolds, his choice of words clearly intended as a rebuke of my haughty preconceptions.

"I never meant to suggest that you or your people were incompetent, General…" I contend despite knowing that I have backed myself into a reductive corner of my own creation.

"It matters not. Let us proceed shall we…" He continues, mercifully sparing me from reflecting further on just how far out of my depths I truly am surrounded by all these beady-eyed spymasters and the stoic special forces automatons ready to execute their orders with indiscriminate prejudice.

All I can do is what I do best, which is listen intently, internalizing the plan he presents to the tribal elders, which he is forced to do in English solely for my benefit. And so I watch as he systematically points out the involved locations, optimal methods, and the Taskforce's required goals, all with what looks to be the retractable car antenna from a 1984 Mitsubishi Galant.

As I understand it, the general's plan goes as such - The hilariously codenamed Sancho Panza (me), will be transported by donkey (an MD 500 Defender helicopter) to the windmill (A migrant processing center on the US-Mexican border). Multiple special forces units will then take their positions around and within the facility before my location is leaked to select persons within the Mexican government long suspected of being on Chase's payroll. Ricardo, who to my surprise is actually a highly trained operative with Mexican intelligence capable of killing a man with the flick of his wrist, will serve as my direct bodyguard, maintaining his cover as a mid-level government flunky throughout. To guarantee that Chase personally appears alongside or close to the much more seasoned hit squad he is bound to dispatch this time around, the leaked story is that I will only be in Mexico for a few more hours before I am whisked away to Lyon, France to give testimony regarding my explosive Los Osos discoveries at Interpol headquarters.

Now, could I have come up with something better than this rehashed airport novel scheme hastily adapted to suit the inflated scope? Almost certainly. I've read Sun Tzu and Joseph Campbell, Niccolò Machiavelli and Bobby Fischer Teaches Chess. Even the best laid plans seldomly survive their execution intact, yet who am I to argue with their collective years of martial experience?

Time flies when you're actively involved in a plot to bring down an international criminal mastermind, so it's close to 3 AM when the strategy finally meeting ends. Not long after I find myself wandering the deserted halls like little Danny Torrance at the Overlook Hotel, a comparison made even more fitting with Ricardo stalking after me with all the unapologetic subtlety of a restless ghost. I consult my second brain once again, weighing the risk to my personal safety against the reward of my future safety, ultimately deciding that the scales are too evenly balanced to dwell on it any further. I am wounded and tired, and despite the 300 empty rooms in this swanky joint I have no place to hang my head and kick off my shoes while I await the breaking of dawn. I decide to go and check on Lauren and Ellie, hoping to find them both still awake, convinced that some time spent with other civilians who are in over their heads will undo the Gordian Knot in my stomach.

I know that something is wrong as soon as I knock on the door and it slides open without further prompting. Ricardo senses something is amiss as well and he quickly grabs my arm, his viselike grip stopping me from going any farther. I watch with slack-jawed astonishment as he effortlessly sheds his timid facade and morphs into a sleek, compact jungle cat before my very eyes, a transformation this is truly terrifying to behold.

This new, spectacularly unnerving iteration of Ricardo presses a finger to his lips, easily pulling me aside to take the lead. I hover over his shoulder as he crouches low and slowly enters the room, but despite the dimness inside I am still able to recognize Ellie's unconscious form slumped over on the floor. I push past Ricardo and rush to her side, lifting her bleeding head and cradling it on my lap.

"Help! Someone help!" I scream as loud as I can. I scream until my voice cracks, until my throat throbs, until my screams are the only thing I have left. The warm blood oozing from Ellie's head wound seeping through my fingers while I struggle to fight back an odyssey's worth of guilty tears.

Ricardo's walkie-talkie suddenly squelches behind me, pulling my soul back into my body. And as I emerge from my fugue state all I am able to hear is one name mentioned over and over. *"Irina."*

My eyes widen in realization and I look around the room, searching for Lauren, but she is gone…

CHAPTER 16

A Rattlesnake Inside The Nowhere Hotel

Ellie still hasn't regained consciousness when a man with a stethoscope hanging around his neck rushes into the room, roughly pushing me aside to check on my cousin's vital signs. While his urgency is greatly appreciated, and assuming that this is the same person who tended to my gunshot wound yesterday, then I can't complain about his methods thus far. But there is just something about seeing someone check for a pulse while dressed in cut-off jean shorts and an 'It's Going *TIBIA* Okay' t-shirt that forces you to question their medical credentials.

"Who are you? Are you a doctor?" I ask dubiously, dispensing with any pleasantries in the face of the unthinkable- That Ellie might succumb to her injury.

"Si." He answers curtly without ever looking up, too inspecting the gaping wound along Ellie's hairline to indulge me further.

But since I am unable to be anything but hypercritical and indifferent to boundaries when I'm feeling helpless, I press him anyway. "Really? Because you're dressed like our Uncle Luca at a family barbecue. Where did you go to medical school?" I demand.

"Stanford. Perhaps you are familiar with it." He claps back while fishing inside his leather Gladstone bag, his arrogance at where he went to school immediately convincing me that he is in fact, a doctor.

As I crane my neck over the man's shoulder to better see what he is doing (and in no way crowding him mind you), the man rattles off a couple of terse sentences in Spanish. When I try to clarify what he said, my giant elevator friend comes in and picks me up, carrying me out of the room.

Unceremoniously deposited outside like an old sofa, I witness Marco barking at the soldiers gathered in the hallway, the rapid-fire cadence of his Spanish and the grim tone of his sentences suggesting that he is on the warpath, may god have mercy on anyone who is not on the same level.

I tap him on the shoulder relentlessly until he finally turns around. "How can I help?" I ask in the most vinegar-soaked voice I'm capable of, my future sore-throat be damned.

"Not now, Nick." He answers irritatedly, unimpressed by my mediocre Clint Eastwood impersonation. "Please let the professionals handle this and just stay out of the way."

His outright dismissal of me is like lighter fluid casually sprinkled on the embers of my dwindling resolve, a catalyst for the foolhardy determination that suddenly flares up inside me. A fire that was lit when I first discovered Chase's cold-hearted desecration of my adopted home, the flames rekindled anew by Irina's unexpected betrayal, and now stoked to wildfire proportions by what I perceive to be the underestimation of my willingness to see this through to the end. No matter the cost. If there is one thing in life that makes us all stronger, it is the unconditional love for another. And when the people you love are hurt or in danger, the cage opens and lets slip the dogs of war.

"Irina has Lauren. So if you have another gun, give it to me now. Otherwise I'll be forced to take the one you have in your hand." I state unflinchingly, leaving no room for further debate.

Marco, seeing the renewed certainty of purpose in my eyes, takes the .380 caliber pistol tucked into his ankle holster and places it in my hand. "Fair enough, amigo. Just try not to shoot anyone you're not supposed to."

As soon as I feel the weight of the gun in my palm I realize I have no idea what to do next. Unlike the rest of the men systematically scouring the deserted hotel for Lauren and Irina, I was not trained for this. But what I lack in tactical skill I more than make up for in gumption. When you are unaware of the rules then you have no idea they even exist, which more often than not leads to some very outside-the-box thinking. In my case this meant simply looking out the window of the closest open hotel room. With an uninterrupted 180 degree bird's-eye view of the resort, I quickly spot Irina dragging Lauren by the arm across the western promenade, hurrying her along at gunpoint towards the service jetty behind a row of dive shops. With Marco nowhere to be found, and deciding that my Spanish is laughable under even the best of circumstances, I eschew informing any of the dozen or so soldiers I pass on my way to the elevator. The language barrier would only slow me down, giving Irina more time to make her escape. But as I jab my thumb against the button over and over, it becomes clear that the elevator will take too long to reach me. My only alternative being this many floors up is to take the stairs. Now I'm not a spry man, and my advanced age has nothing to do with that. I was an academic by trade but I've always been one by inclination, so on the whole there was never any reason to exercise beyond those restorative constitutionals I'm so fond of. I know that a mad dash down to the lobby from 30 stories up will tax my body beyond anything I have ever experienced before, almost certainly killing me with a heart attack in the process. But I cannot let Irina leave the resort with Lauren in tow, deliberately taken to be used as a chess piece against me. *Here goes everything* I think to myself as I push open the ominous swing door that leads out to the landing. If the road to hell is paved with good intentions, then the stairway to heaven is a broken escalator across the vastness of human uncertainty. But heroes never say die, especially when they know that dying is what is expected of them. And with that in mind I take the first step into the abyss, hands held in prayer, but also with my fingers crossed to hedge my bets. If love makes you stronger, perhaps it makes you more durable as well…

I'm already drenched in sweat after tackling only two flights of stairs, but I console myself with the Judeo-Christian certainty that if I die on the way down, it's an express trip back up. Because my demise will have happened while doing something intentionally heroic. And if that doesn't guarantee me an audience to air out my grievances with whatever I meet up there, then karmic comeuppance is a multi-denominational lie. If an existential crisis isn't warranted in times of crisis then when is it?

I eventually reach the bottom after who knows how long, out of breath and close to passing out, yet otherwise "miraculously" unscathed. Much like every nation in existence, my body has seemingly extended itself a line of credit to be collected at a (hopefully) much later date. But while I am eager to exploit my borrowed time, things look a lot different at ground level. I dart out of the hotel tower and run towards the area where I last saw them, but the snake's path to the jetty that was so clear from above is now obscured by the picturesque promenade's Toltec Empire inspired landscaping, with all the serpent-columns-and-peculiar Chac Mool figures conspiring to present a difficult to navigate maze. Everywhere I turn I run headlong into giant animal-human hybrid statues or dormant ATM machines, and with each new dead end I encounter, the odds of me reaching Lauren in time to make a difference skew further and further away from my favor.

I am aware that there is no such thing as a photographic memory, at least not in the way that Hollywood has been presenting it to moviegoers since the 'talkies'. But there is something called eidetic memory, which is for all intents and purposes, the same thing. And while I don't remember every little snippet of information I've come across throughout the years, I do tend to remember most of what I've read, although it's usually contingent on if I found the topic mildly interesting or tangentially useful. Celestial navigation was something I was reading about last year when I was seriously considering buying a sail boat, but then Ellie convinced me to use that money to move to Los Osos instead. I've retained enough information on the subject to know that by my dead reckoning, all I have to do is look up at the sun and back down to follow the signs. I spot one such sign etched on a large wooden arrow nailed to a post and pointing left - This Way To Jetty.

I reach the small pier just in time to see Irina discard the mooring rope onto the dock, kicking off the dock so as to allow **My Sailvation** to slowly drift toward the open waters of the bay. For a moment I seriously consider running to the end of the marina and leaping onto the boat, but a Rube Goldberg-esq series of events that ends in me accidentally shooting Lauren or myself in the face flashes in my mind's eye and stops me cold. I raise my gun and aim it at Irina, convinced I will have better luck putting my newfound sharpshooter skills to task instead. When in dire straits it's always money for nothing and the evil chicks for free. I close one eye and immediately have her backside in my sights; I can end this all with but a single squeeze. And that's when a new series of images suddenly race through my head like a zoetrope but with sound, some of them instances where Irina was kind to me, some of them where she flirted, and the rest where she literally saved my life. She was right, it's one thing to shoot up a paper enemy, but another thing entirely to do it when it counts. My hesitation costs me everything. Irina sees the gun, flashing me a knowing smile before yanking a sobbing Lauren up by the hair and positioning her as a human shield.

"Look down." Irina yells as the speedboat continues to drift farther away. "I left you my number."

I pick up the cellphone I find lying a few feet away, my moral compass in shambles, spinning wildly every which way but true north. How can someone so beautiful on the outside be so ugly on the inside? I would have trusted her with my life, but instead she took my heart and is now holding it hostage. By the time I pull myself together Irina has started the engine, leaving me in her wake.

CHAPTER 17

<u>(Standing On) The Dock of Disarray</u>

"Don't tell anyone you have this. If you do, we will know. We have eyes everywhere. I will contact you with further instructions. xoxo - Irina "

That's the message that pops up on the screen of the burner phone as soon as I turn it on. The hugs and kisses are a particularly cruel touch. If I wasn't fully convinced that Irina was a villain before, those taunting accoutrements certainly drive the message home. I had the opportunity to shoot her in the face but I just couldn't bring myself to pull the trigger, and now poor sweet Lauren is paying the price for my spinelessness. I feel like an essential organ has been carved out of my side with a rusty scalpel plucked from between Irina's ample bosom. I am deflated and less than for having allowed the woman I love to be taken, and all I want to do is hand the phone over to Marco when I hear him rushing up behind me. But I know I must do as the message says if I ever want to see Lauren again, and so I quickly slip the burner phone into my pocket before he can see it.

"What happened, Nick? Where is La Xtabay?" Marco asks, referencing the Yucatec Mayan folklore tale about a demonic femme fatale who preys upon easily exploitable men like me.

"She got away." I answer dejectedly, which is true. "I didn't get here in time." I add, which isn't.

Seeing the sorry state that I am in, Marco places a hand on my shoulder in an effort to comfort me. "You did all you could, amigazo. Do not despair too easily. We will find them. And when we do I will personally feed that traitorous temptress her own heart as payment for stealing yours."

"Thank you, my friend." I nod somberly, allowing the guilt and shame I feel for keeping secrets from someone that sincerely seems to value our friendship to be mistaken for impotent concern.

"Come, let us return to the hotel. You are needed elsewhere right now." Marco urges as he guides me away from the edge of the jetty.

I takes a few seconds to realize what he means. But when I do that realization hits me with the same amount of force as the bullet that pierced my stomach. The fact that I could even forgot about Ellie and her life threatening injury, even amidst Lauren's abduction, sends me into an emotional tailspin.

I can't think straight. This is all too much for one person to handle. My vision blurs around the edges and my thoughts unravel just before darkness comes and takes me…

CHAPTER 18

Estranged Bedfellows

I sit up gasping, and as soon as I open eyes I am immediately assaulted by a canopy of bright florescent lighting that floods my corneas, effectively rendering me flash blind. Temporarily robbed of my sight, I am forced to attune to my other senses. My shirt is completely soaked through with sweat, wet and heavy as it hangs on my shoulders. My stomach feels tight, like there is a rubber compress filled with scalding water taped to the skin, sending wave upon wave of burning pain that resonates throughout my bloated torso. I press my hand down on my abdomen, and everything below my ribcage is wet and the sticky, my fingers smelling like quarters when I bring them up to shield my face. I desperately grab at every stray thought racing around my throbbing head, hoping to assemble a single coherent image in my mind. But it's a fool's errand. I am far too disoriented to be of any use to myself. All I know for certain is that I have no idea where I am and that scares me. But as tears born of confusion and frustration slowly restore my vision, I see a shape that I decide belongs to a woman enter the room. She is wearing some kind of white uniform, and as my sight improves to within spitting distance of what it usually is, I can see that it is a nurse's uniform. I look around the room with clearer eyes this time, and between the green walls and all the monitors around me, I am able to deduce that I am in a hospital. But then again, one can never be too sure.

"Excuse me, miss." I address the young nurse politely as she checks my chart. "Is this a hospital?"

"Si. El hospital." She answers as she causally empties out my embarrassingly full bedpan.

Once she is done with the tasks that specifically pertain to me, she pulls aside the curtain slid down the center of the room. To my surprise, Ellie is in the next bed, her head bandaged tightly, with an IV drip hooked up to her arm. She looks so very frail, although I try to rationalize it as me not being used to seeing her in such a languid state, having become accustomed to her gregarious, perpetually in motion demeanor throughout the years. But I have read a few medical text books in my day, back when I thought I wanted to be the next Robin Cook, and while I am not an expert by any stretch of even my own imagination, I know that the beeping EKG machine monitoring her heartbeat is spiking along evenly at a rate of 80 beats per minute, which means that she is in stable condition.

"Has she woken up yet?" I ask the nurse as I swing my legs over to sit on the edge of my bed, the sudden draft that tickles my nether regions informing me that I'm not wearing the clothes I passed out in after all, and that I'm actually dressed in nothing but a hospital gown split down the back. The nurse turns to answer me, and I quickly cross my legs to prevent her from getting an eyeful.

"I am sorry, señor. That kind of information is only to be given to family members." She says as she starts toward the door.

"I *am* family. She is my cousin. Mi prima." I divulge, pretending that I do not notice the curious expression on her face as she tries to ascertain why I look like I'm sitting on a pineapple.

"The doctor shall be in shortly. You may ask him these questions then." She finally says, currently looking all too eager to get free of the wacky old gringo.

"One last thing, por favor. Where are my clothes? Mis pantalones?" I ask as she is halfway out the door.

"En el armario." She replies, pointing at the closet built into the wall.

I walk over to the closet and pull the doors open. Sure enough, I find all my clothes neatly stacked within, with my wallet and the burner phone inside a zip-loc bag set on top. I retrieve the phone, and just as I suspected, there is already a message waiting.

"Be at this location at 16:00 tomorrow. Come alone. xoxo - Irina " the message says, along with a set coordinates in the form of a red pin drop icon on a digital map of Quintana Roo. Again with the hugs and kisses? This woman is the human equivalent of a Dirty Screwdriver - a glass of 192 proof Polish vodka with a splash of orange juice and two dashes of cinnamon sadism.

After I get dressed I walk over to Ellie's bedside and take her hand. "Don't worry, Cuz. One way or another, this all ends tomorrow." I assure her before I peel off the EKG patch pasted to her forearm, which causes her heart monitor to flatline, setting off a code blue alarm.

CHAPTER 19

Journey Into Mystery

I pull the privacy curtain shut and scramble under my bed, allowing my plan to unfold. A few minutes later a handful of nurses responding to the alarm burst in with a crash cart and crowd Ellie's bed. They are immediately followed into the room by two armed soldiers, men that I had correctly assumed were standing guard outside the door. One of them pulls the curtain to the side and starts to yell at the other in breakneck Spanish when he finds my bed empty. But in their panic, neither of them thinks to check under the bed. I watch until both pairs of boots have run out of the room before sliding out from my hiding spot, and with all the commotion of trying to figure out why the monitor is saying my cousin flatlined, no one even notices me slip out of the room.

I pass the nurse's station with my head down to conceal my face, seriously wishing I had my Phillies cap with me right now. As I look up to see if the woman behind the counter notices me, I catch a glimpse of a calendar hanging on the wall behind her. My second brain flicks my frontal lobe as I rush past, but before I can interpret the prompt I hear the sound of hurried footsteps coming from around the corner. I reach the fire escape without incident just as Marco and his men arrive at my hospital room. I feel the pangs of self-recrimination when

I see the worry stamped in capital letters on his usually grim face, but I force it back down to be dealt with later. Perhaps in the taxi cab I'm sure I'll have to get into at some point, because what better place is there for regretting ones decisions than in the backseat of a cab? Speaking of taxi cabs, do I even have any money? I check my wallet. *It's empty.* So far this "adventure" has forced me to become many things with which I am uncomfortable with, but the thought of adding thief to the ever growing list affects me on a level I'm unprepared for. Maybe it's because in my relentless pursuit of bringing Chase to justice, I find myself acting more and more like him. Could it be that Nietzsche was right? Have I been gazing too long into the abyss that it has now gazed back into me? Yet another thing I'll have to unpack with the shrink I'm sure to need if I survive tomorrow. *Tomorrow.* The word suddenly rests heavy on my shoulders. But why? And then I have the lightbulb moment my second brain foreshadowed.

I check the message on the phone again, but this time I consider the date it was sent. May *31st*. My mind flashes back to the calendar at the nurses station. The page was on *June…* Meaning that when I passed out I lost a whole day! Irina isn't expecting me tomorrow because today *is* tomorrow. Great, so she's expecting me at 4pm *today*, which if this burner phone is to believed is just a few hours from now. Don't panic, Nick. It's only Lauren's life at stake. You'll find another wonderful woman that loves you for you. I hear that neophobic former English professors with an inflated sense of self-worth despite crippling writer's block are in high demand these days. Of course there's always the question of what will happen to her children. Little Todd and the other one. But they're both young enough, they'll get over it eventually. I think Lauren mentioned that her ex was dating someone…

My goodness these are a lot of stairs! I sure am getting my steps in today. Okay, focus. I need money to get to where I need to be. From what I've been led to believe by the youth of today, the internet is the answer to all of life's problems, and thankfully this burner phone has wireless fidelity. And so I do the previously unthinkable and google 'Pickpocketing for dummies', confident that I should at least be able to learn the basics iterated in the first video before I get to the bottom of the stairwell.

But as I step out into that familiar blistering heat, the glare of the sun stapling my eyelids shut, the only information I have retained is a jingle for Mexican laundry soap. How do people live like this? Having to wait for… Oh, wait… There's a skip button. Was that always there?

Fine, I guess I'm going to have to just wing this whole thief thing, necessity usually breeds innovation after all. First, I have to choose my mark. Someone smaller, easily intimidated by older people walking up to them outside of hospitals, preferably a child wearing expensive clothing like Levis jeans. Yes, I am fully aware of how that sounds… Is Levis even considered a designer brand in this part of the world? And how much should I even steal from this hypothetical child? Do I just take everything the kid has? I'm not even sure where I am let alone how much a taxi will cost to get to where I need to be… Who knew stealing from children would be so hard?

I am still deep in thought, mapping out my pocket change money heist to the absolute letter, when I feel a tap on my shoulder. I whirl around, coming face to face with Marco causally smoking a cigarette. From his relaxed and unsurprised manner, it's clear he's been waiting for me.

"Hola, amigo! This isn't…" I stammer in a clumsy attempt to conceal my true intentions. "It was such a lovely day outside so I thought I might go for a walk. Get some fresh air."

"En realidad?" He asks with a raised eyebrow, obviously amused. "So you just decided to go for a walk even if your beloved cousin is upstairs and still unconscious?" He continuous, visibly eager to hear how I try to talk my way out of this.

"You know me. Always the tourist. Never met a mysterious city I wasn't chomping at the bit to explore." I explain, not ready to abandon my ruse just yet.

"Ah, si si. Cancun is truly a puzzle to be unlocked by the people that can appreciate its complexities." He nods in agreement, finishing off his cigarette and stamping it out under foot.

"Took the words right out of my mouth. I'm just so blessed to be able to experience all of this beauty and…" I agree, sweeping my open palm over the unobstructed view of all the American fast-food chain restaurants that line the congested highway. "…and you're not buying any of this are you?" I ask, realizing how stupid I sound.

"I'm a professional spy, amigo. Did you really think you could, how you say, shake me?" He replies, his subsequent laughter reminding me yet again of just how out of my depths I am and will always be. "So… Have there been any new messages on the phone Irina left you?" He asks.

CHAPTER 20

My Life in Ancient Ruins

As it turns out Marco found the burner phone almost immediately after I passed out, and after reading the message, he arranged for Ellie and I to be airlifted by chopper to a hospital in Cancun, a mere 80 or so miles from the coordinates sent by Irina. Even though he apologized for allowing me to believe I had actually pulled off my clever escape for as long as he did, I don't think I will ever forgive him for standing by while I grunted down twenty flights of stairs in service of the superfluous. I completely understand that the ruse was necessary to sell Chase's people, imbedded in who knows how many government institutions, on the verisimilitude of my hospital bed exodus, but it has become evident to me that I cannot trust a word that comes out of Marco's mouth. He's a spy, and I would assume that being a good one requires an exceptional degree of emotional detachment. I was a fool to think that our relationship transcended the strict symbiosis of handler and asset. I know my role, the part I am expected to shut up and play without complaint, and I will draw upon every John le Carré trope I remember to hit my marks and play it well.

So here I am, three hours after my "great escape", sitting in the backseat of a green Volkswagen taxi cab that Marco has borrowed from the local police impound, one of his most trusted men dressed inconspicuously in a white polo shirt behind the wheel. I try and maintain my composure as best I can as the car slowly pulls up into the parking lot, the heat working in my favor as I wipe away the nervous sweat on my brow. But as soon as the breathtaking Mayan Ruins of Tulum come into view, the writer in my takes over. I catch a glimpse of the undercover agent's wireless earpiece and my stomach does a somersault, because even though Marco has assured me that he has kept the circle small, with only a handful of agents aware of the mini-operation he has cobbled together at the last second, I now know with absolute certainty that I am expendable, even to the only friend I thought I had here.

I pay the undercover agent and he makes a show of giving me my change, but in keeping with the character I have decided on playing, that of the magnanimous American tourist, I tell him to keep the change - all three pesos of it. Eat your heart out Marlon Brando, and this year's Golden Globe for best actor in a comedy or musical goes to…

I must admit that I feel like somewhat of a celebrity as soon as I step out of the car and into the stale swampy air, even though the people swamping me are less interested in my autograph than they are in plying their 'I Love Tulum' souvenirs or humbly offering up their services as the best tour guides my American dollars can buy. If this were any other day of my life I might have gladly hired one of them… As it stands I know next to nothing about the history of this place except for that, as opposed to other Mayan cities that practiced human sacrifice, this place celebrated the god of life, Ah Puch, and so people were spared. Thus the irony of dying here as a human sacrifice is not lost on me…

My pocket vibrates, it's the burner phone with new instructions - Make your way to the top of el castillo on the cliff. I hope you are alone. Lauren is waiting.

I find veiled threats to be more terrifying than explicitly stated ones, because the unknown gives your mind permission to go to places it otherwise wouldn't dare to. And now that I know for sure I am being watched, every face in the crowd must become an adversary. Although the instructions from my enemies are now clear, the instructions from my so-called allies are becoming less so. I was told by Marco to identify Chase, then remove Lauren from harm's way, and then duck. Simple enough on the surface, yet it is still a plan formulated on the assumption that I naturally posses the skill to pull something of that caliber off. Which nothing in my history here in Mexico even comes close to suggesting. I may be a lazy writer, but that doesn't mean I can't recognize lazy writing.

I suppose the root of my overall discomfort is that I understand my enemies on a base level, they have clear cut motives for luring me here. But my allies' ultimate intentions are not as crystal clear for allowing me to come in the first place, at least not when it comes to me and Lauren. Hence my mind lighting up like a pinball machine with questions as I touch upon them. What is their endgame? How far will the shadow cabinet go to see this through? But also, to what lengths will they go if it all goes wrong today? I know I am essentially expendable but does that expendability extend to Lauren as well? If we die here how will they explain it away on the news? What talking points will be fed to news anchors by that creep Lucas Garza? Disappearance by misadventure most likely, or maybe something more salacious. If you're going to lie, lie so big that sensationalism overshadows the truth. I looked into Chase's eyes back in Los Osos and saw the man inside the monster, his congeniality may have been a mask, but it made for a clear delineation between the two aspects of the man. With the people that have used me at every turn, their actions decided by committee and populist voting, the line moves so often it might as well not even exist. A line drawn in the sand can always be redrawn every time the tide washes it away. Because you always have the luxury of changing your mind when the consequences happen to someone else. When it's always someone else in the crosshairs of accountability you can afford to be aloof in your innovation. I know I'm overanalyzing everything once again as I traverse yet another flight of stairs to reach the zenith of the castle, they may be ancient steps but stairs are still stairs to any man, especially one of my advanced age. I won't apologize for having an analytical mind. When so much of the literature I've studied for over fifty years of my life is designed to be open to interpretation, how can I not predicate ever forward momentum that I make with questions?

I stumble to the top of Ah Puch's temple, out of breath and on my knees, ready to collapse without any answers to the questions that plague me. With the most important question at this point being: Has everyone forgotten that I was shot not too long ago? Stope making me climb stairs!

Through the sting of my sweat I see the woman that stowed the bleeding on the speedboat and probably saved my life. She is still the perfect combination of beautiful and sexy, a one-two punch to the chilled chin of hyper-masculinity meant to obfuscate her deadlier tendencies. But Irina is alone, without Lauren like she promised. My fists clench in rage, huffing and puffing to compensate for the words I want to say but cannot muster in my exhaustion. She lied. I lied as well of course, I am not alone, Marco and his inner circle of Elliot Ness Untouchables are somewhere around here too. But unlike *her* deceit, mine is caped in a cloak of righteousness.

Irina smiles at me, daring me to make the next move. I now that Marco has vowed to kill this woman, am I capable of the same? The back of my hand brushes against the gun Marco taped to my inner thigh as I struggle to my feet, an insurance policy in case things go sideways. Which they always do. I was never sure I could put a bullet in her head until just now.

CHAPTER 21
Speak of The Devil and He Doth Appear

Chase emerges from the darkest depths of Au Puch's temple with Lauren pulled tightly to his side. I can't see it, but her body language lets me know that he has a gun pressed against her back. Ever the consummate showman, it's the kind of entrance you would expect from someone like him, an entrance reserved exclusively for James Bond villains. Lauren's eyes are pregnant with tears, and while her distress does send a pang of guilt shooting up my spine, what's at the forefront of my thoughts is how he is a lot smaller than I remember. I was never sure how it would feel if we ever came face to face again, but pity was the last thing I would have expected to be my primary emotion. He has a full salt and pepper beard, and just the knowledge that he hasn't been able to shave since his prison break somehow makes him seem less intimidating to me.

Life certainly is partial to its symmetry - Which is why here we are again, two men from vastly different walks of life, finally confronting each other after a week's worth of caustic build up. Feelings-wise, it's pretty much just like the first time we danced, only now it's atop the ruins of an ancient Mayan city with the whole of Mexico's wide open expanses surrounding us… And my nemesis looks like a caged animal, or worse, a circus bear on a tiny bicycle going through the motions.

Despite the unfathomable magnitude of Chase's resources, here is here standing before me looking like everyone's black sheep uncle. My boogeyman has chosen to step out from the shadows into the light, and as it turns out, he's just a man. And unlike actual monsters, men can bleed.

"Hello, Nick. How do you like the view?" Chase asks trying to be clever, our eyes already locked in a battle of wills that could decided the outcome of this encounter before it even truly begins.

We size each other up for the first time since the Los Osos incident, with him still unable to shed the carefully curated persona he has crafted over the years for public consumption, flashing me a smile meant for toothpaste commercials or donate to my gubernatorial campaign billboards. In direct contrast to that, my bared teeth cannot even begin to adequately encapsulate just how much I despise this man's stupid face. This has been personal for the two of us a good long while now, but whoever took it in that direction is inconsequential. Only one of us is walking away from this.

"Hello, Chase. I'd really appreciate it if you'd let go of my girlfriend now." I answer as casually as possible, intent on dealing with him on equal footing this time around.

"I'll let her go soon enough." Chase promises amicably. "But in what shape is completely up to you." He quickly adds, his voice taking on a more ominous tone. "She was only ever a means to get you here." He openly admits, acknowledging Lauren's function as mere collateral damage to keep our little transcontinental game of cat and mouse interesting. Hubris is 'the silent killer of all great men and women of achievement.' An actor said that once. Fitting as I play the role of instigator. "You're risking an awful lot just for little old me." I answer without missing a beat, determined to highlight the absurdity of his vendetta. "Wouldn't your time be better spent in a non-extradition country getting extensive facial reconstructive surgery?"

"Have you ever had a pebble in your shoe, Nick?" Chase asks musingly. "You don't think it's a big deal at first. But as the day goes on…" He continues, trailing off for added emphasis.

But before Chase can continue with his obviously premeditated metaphor, he is forced to stop when he sees a man bundled in a filthy poncho, hunched over and hobbling up the steps, a garland of flowers twined around one arm as he slowly makes his way through our little Mexican standoff. As the man walks past us I look down and notice the army issue boots he is wearing, immediately understanding that this is part of a larger plan that Marco has purposely kept from me.

I have no choice but to play along with this subterfuge, compartmentalizing my emotions for fear of tipping Chase or Irina off and plunging an already volatile situation past the point of no return.

"How about we handle this like men for once, Chase?" I blurt out, keeping all the attention on me.

"What do you have in mind, professor? Fisticuffs at midnight?" He asks mockingly, but says it in such a way as to suggest to me that I may be on the right track by challenging his virility.

"We're old men and our pugilist days are long behind us. We should end this like the gentlemen that we both claim to be. How about a duel?" I propose, finely tuning the rhetoric leading up to my proposition so as to capitalize on his outdated idea of masculinity. And if in the process, I allow Marco and his men some time to enact whatever scheme they have concocted, better the devil you're chummy with than the one you aren't.

"Speak for yourself. I'm in the prime of my life." He objects. "But a duel does sound mildly intriguing…" And then he professes, nibbling on the bait.

"This has to end at some point, Chase. I would assume your revenge against me would be much more gratifying if you exacted it on equal terms. Surely a man of your position didn't get to where he is by taking the easy way." I cajole, remembering from my research at the Los Ossos public library that he started from the bottom. And so I use that information against him to evoke any nostalgia he may have for past accomplishments during his initial rise to power. And judging by the twinkle of memory in his eyes I can see that it's working. "You have made a valid point, professor. You must have been a very good teacher once upon a time. But now it's my turn to teach *you* a lesson. My pistol is at the ready, but Irina still has yours. How about this then, *old man*? A counter proposal if you will. Take your gun back from Irina and I will gladly have that duel with you…" He says, throwing down a challenge of his own, one that he believes will be impossible for me to accomplish.

My eyes dart from Chase to Irina, and then from Chase to Lauren. He's right of course. Irina is a a highly trained operative, and there is no way I can disarm her by myself. But thankfully I have discovered that in this country, I am never alone.

"Shoot him." I whisper into the button on my lapel, just loud enough for the man in the poncho to hear me. I have not been provided with any sort of listening device with which anyone can hear me mind you, but Chase doesn't know that, and he reacts accordingly. If the universe has designated me the wrench in everyone's machinery, then it's about time that I started abusing the privilege.

The feeble old man throws off his poncho to reveal that it is Marco in disguise. Something I suspected to be the case and was in fact banking on. A friend in deed, is a friend indeed. Even if you have to force said friend's hand every so often.

The pillar next to Chase's head suddenly explodes in a spray of dust and rock, temporarily blinding him just as the rifle shot that punctured the column echoes throughout the entire compound. Did I know that was going to happen? Not specifically that. But I knew that *something* would.

A rapid-fire skirmish breaks out around the temple as almost every single person in the compound is suddenly revealed to be an agent of one side or the other. Within the initial confusion and its ensuing chaos, I use the opportunity to spring forward like a tightly coiled Jack in the box, knocking Chase down to the hard limestone floor, sending his gun skating over the edge of them temple and tumbling down into crashing waves below us. I immediately wrench Lauren free of his grasp, but in my haste to remove her from harm's way as quickly as possible, I forget about the greater threat.

"Not so fast, Nick!" She shouts, freeing my pistol she from her waistband and swinging it in my direction. She has me dead to rights, and so I close my eyes and wait for my story to abruptly end. But to my surprise, she flips the gun around and holds it out towards me. "You're gonna need this."

I am too dumfounded to take her offering at first, but when I notice she and Marco exchange a quick nod, all the seemingly disparate pieces fly towards each other like magnets with opposite polarities. They planned this! The animosity between the two of them, Irina's supposed betrayal of the shadow cabinet, they planned all of it from the beginning! My mind is spinning so fast that the heart struggles to synch up with the head. All the time and effort that went into this, the unwavering dedication to the ruse. Layer upon layer of lies, with contingencies for contingencies. The scope of it all is just so staggering, with both their performances so convincing that it's now Chase's turn to be confused when I take the gun from Irina and point it directly at Marco.

"Nick, what the heck are you doing?!" Lauren gasps, asking out loud what everyone else is thinking.

I ignore the question, images of Ellie lying unconscious in a hospital bed flashing faster and faster in my mind like a comic book flung open by the wind, with every ensuing page inked in a deeper red.

"Who did it? Which one of you put my cousin in the hospital?" I demand, my aim alternating between Marco and Irina for the whole world to see. I'm well past the point of caring though. The heart has caught up to the mind, and both believe that it's time for a reckoning.

"That's what these people do, Nick. They can't be trusted. Neither can I, but at least I'm honest about being a liar." Chase interjects before Irina shuts him up with a well placed boot to the face.

"I understand your anger, Nick. I truly do." Marco says sympathetically, slowly approaching me with both hands up in the air. "And I am sorry for what had to happen to Ellie. Please give me the gun and we can talk about it later. Let's just put this *cabron* behind bars first."

Seeing the sincerity in his eyes, hearing the earnestness in his voice, I almost do what he's asking of me and set the gun right on his open palm. But his use of the word 'Had' bothers me. 'What *had* to happen to Ellie'. No one *has* to do anything. We *choose* to do things. We are the ultimate the sum of all our choices, and I choose not to be swayed by another performance from a master manipulator. I choose to take a step back and raise my gun anew…

"I'm saying this because I really do like you, Nick. But I won't say it again. Point the gun where it should be pointed." Irina warns, her eyes narrowing with unpleasant intent.

"I am." I answer coldly as I flip off the safety, so consumed by my outrage that I fail to notice Chase until it's too late.

He scrambles up to his feet and slips between Marco and Irina, grabbing my wrist. As we struggle for control of the gun it suddenly goes off, the bullet striking Marco in the neck. He clutches his throat as he crumples to the ground, blood spurting through the gaps in this fingers. I knee Chase as hard as I can in the testicles, hearing a satisfying wheeze as all the air in his lungs leaves his body. I instinctively sweep his leg and throw him down, his head hitting the limestone with a loud smack and knocking him unconscious.

I turn my attention back to Marco, watching helplessly as he slowly and surly chokes to death on a mouthful of blood while Irina cradles his head in her arms. He looks up at me as she strokes his hair back, with an accusatory stare that never wavers even as the light in his eyes dim.

Irina screams at the sky when his head falls back and hangs limp against her embrace. It's the kind of guttural wail I'd like to imagine Lauren let out after I was shot, but I know that probably wasn't the case. What I'm hearing is the sound you make for true love lost, a once-in-a-lifetime connection where you are so intertwined with the other person that even your bones have coiled around and fused to each other. She will feel his absence for the rest of her life, ruining herself for every person that comes after. His death will leave a gash on her soul, a jagged line marking the before and after, a fault line between the BC and the AD in a secret alphabet of rumination.

None of what I have just said may even be true at all. They are simply the things I *believe* to be true in the moment. The only thing I know for certain is that his death hits me hard. I barely knew the man, and what little he allowed me to know of himself was most probably a lie. Even if that is the case though, I do feel that I shall know the loss of him immensely. Our time spent together akin to sharing a foxhole during wartime. No matter how tumultuous, they are memories that must be reflected on, mileposts on the long and lonely highway to becoming a better human being.

My first stop is clear. I want to approach Irina, to lay a comforting hand on her shoulder, to make her aware that I share in her grief. But even though I am all but certain that it was Chase's finger that pulled the trigger, I am not sure that I would be welcomed with anything other than hostility right now. But my hesitation and uncertainty regarding what should happen next is rendered moot when the decision is taken out of my hands. Led by the man who drove me here, a squad of soldiers in tactical gear storms the temple, the muzzles of every single one of their FX-05 Xiuhcoatl assault rifles aimed at my face as they force me down onto my stomach next to the still unconscious Chase.

CHAPTER 22
The Scapegoat

"Everything is going to be okay." I assure Lauren while my right cheek is pressed hard against the dusty limestone of the temple floor, the knee of someone much stronger than I digging between my shoulder blades. She reaches out to me as two soldiers haul me up to my feet, but before I can reach back my wrists are restrained tightly behind my back with a zip-tie.

Although I am unable to see her, I can hear Irina's voice. "You killed him." She says over and over, the words spilling out of her mouth like acid. "You killed Marco…"

I have to assume she means me. A part of me wants to point out that it takes two to wrestle with a gun, and that we would never have even been in this tragic position to begin with if she and Marco had just been honest with me about their plans from the start. But my protests would simply be salt and vinegar rubbed into a fresh wound if she does hold me responsible for her pain, a band-aid for the bullet hole that shattered her heart if she doesn't.

It takes all the self-control I still miraculously posses not to struggle as the two soldiers "escort" me to the bottom of the temple by the armpits, the toe caps of my shoes barely scuffing the ground as they all but carry me down the stone steps. But the unceremonious way with which they are manhandling me suggests that I am no longer in the good graces of the Mexican government.

"You've got the wrong guy!" I finally insist, beseeching no one in particular as I actively scour the faces of every grime-faced man I pass to ascertain just who is in charge here. "If I could just talk to your General he can clear this whole thing up for you…"

But everyone I plead my case to simply ignores me, which is probably for the best right now. If they truly believe that I killed their beloved El Capitan, then I'm lucky to still be alive. But for how much longer remains to be seen. There are countless ways a man can be killed on the road to absolution.

I frantically look around for any sign of Chase's whereabouts, begrudgingly coming to the conclusion that he may be the only person outside of Lauren that can vindicate me. She will be easily dismissed as a woman standing by her man, but an enemy's confirmation of innocence, that would be undeniable. Whether he wants to or not is beside the point right now, it is a bridge I can only cross when I get to it. But he is nowhere to be seen, seemingly having vanished into thin air despite still being unconscious when the troops stormed the castle. This could mean one of two things: They have him in custody, or he has escaped yet again. And if he somehow managed to escape with a handful of sniper rifles trained on him, then I'll have to accept that he is untouchable.

The two soldiers shove me into the back of an armored car waiting of us at the bottom, and to my horror I see that it's the same vehicle where they intend to deposit a gurney covered in a white sheet. Once Marco's dead body is secured inside, I see Irina on the arm of that insidious little rodent-man, Lucas Garza. He comforts her in the way that I had wanted to, gently dabbing the tears from her eyes with a monogrammed handkerchief and whispering his condolences in her ear. He keeps her forehead pressed against the nape of his neck, preventing her from looking up and seeing the gloating smile on his face. A victorious smile gleefully reserved just for me. It was never about catching Chase as far as he was concerned, it was only about beating me.

"You know this wasn't my fault, you scoundrel. Where is Chase?" I demand, kicking my foot out in an attempt to mar his self-satisfied face. But it is a futile gesture of defiance since he remains safely out of my reach for now.

"I hope Mexico has been hospitable to you so far, *Professor* Sanders. Because after what you have done here today, you are never ever leaving." He crows in triumph, his words intended to be the nail in my proverbial coffin as she helps Irina into the vehicle and personally shuts the doors behind her.

With Irina sitting right across from me, our car ride to parts unknown only to me is uncomfortable both in the literal sense as well as the figurative. I attempt to tell her how sorry I am for Marco, but each time I open my mouth to speak her steely gaze sews it back shut. A person has never seen true hate until they have seen their own reflection in the eyes of a person that truly hates them.

I feel the ground underneath us suddenly shift, the smooth meander of asphalt abruptly giving way to the uneven and rugged terrain of the desert. The driver slams on the breaks and I am pitched forward, bouncing off the chainlink bulkhead back onto my bench.

"What's going on?" I ask as I rub my smarting ear against my shoulder, helplessly bound and unable to keep the crawling panic out of my voice.

My eyes widen with understanding as Irina reaches behind her back and pulls out a gun, slowly raising it up until the deadly weapon is only a few feet from my face. Staring down the barrel I easily recognize it as the same pistol that I took with me to the Tulum Ruins. The same gun that killed Marco.

CHAPTER 23

<u>Living Dead Man</u>

My second brain hurriedly takes over and ejects my consciousness outside of my body, in an act of self-preservation similar to what happened on the beach, when I was also certain I was about to die. My sentient viewpoint becomes akin to a lizard on a window pane, cold-blooded and aloof, accepting that poetic justice is a warm gun meant for someone else but now aimed at me.

"Anything you would like to profess, *professor?*" Irina asks, a finality in her voice that I can hear and understand, but am unable to connect with on an emotional level.

I read a theory in a Richard Lazarus book where he posits that humans respond to experiences cognitively first, emotionally second, and physically last. And the way I have been responding to a gun pointed at my head leads me to believe there is more than a nugget of truth in that. I am unable to say or do anything, as in control of my body as a puppeteer would be a puppet severed of all its strings. I am a disembodied

floating head, reliving the entirety of its life in the blink of an eye, attaching emotions to the multitude of memories filling up the grooves on my fingertips before circumstances snap my fingers together for the last time. Since one and two of said theory are accounted for, the way is now open for the physical response to my impending death. A bullet in the head, good as dead… I am as ready as I will ever be for what comes next.

I watch, from the outside looking in, as Irina pulls the trigger. The muzzle flashes brightly inside the darkened troop hold, the click of the hammer the most deafening sound I have ever heard in my life. My consciousness is immediately dragged back into my body, and I brace myself for the bullet's impact to my cranium. I didn't feel it the first time I was shot, and I just chalked that up to my body being in the throes of extreme shock. But surprisingly, I feel no pain now as well. How death must truly end all sensation… But then a bead of sweat trickles down my brow, and I slowly come to the realization that I am not dead at all. I open my eyes, one before the hesitant other, squinting out in confusion. The barrel is still there, still aimed at my face. But my head remains conversely intact.

As I prod my forehead in disbelief, still feeling around for the bullet's entry point, the body on the gurney suddenly sits up straight. Still draped in the white sheet, the reanimated corpse reminds me of a 13 year old wearing a hastily assembled Halloween costume. So I do what any sane person would do when faced with the impossible, I start screaming. Irina breaks out into roaring laughter, drowning out my shrieks as she pulls the sheet off like a magician's assistant presenting a captivated audience with the prestige.

A very much alive Marco greets me affably, grinning from ear to ear as if it was utterly ridiculous of me to have believed him to be stone-cold dead just a few seconds ago. *"Hola,* Nick. *Qué pasó?"*

"How…" Is the only word I manage to squeak out, with the rest of my thoughts still backed up in bumper to bumper traffic on the Schuylkill Expressway.

Irina holds up the gun in her hand before sliding out the clip and showing it to me. "Blanks." She reveals gleefully.

"But... but..." I stammer, a quivering finger pointing out the blood all over Marco's neck.

"Corn syrup and food dye. A little... what is the term? Ah yes. A little movie magic." He explains. "Your Hollywood was one once upon a time a part of my Mexico you know." He adds matter-of-factly before promptly licking the fake blood off of his fingers.

I don't know what to think anymore. Is this even real life? I'm honestly waiting for the director to yell cut so I can discover that I've been one of those method actors this entire time. Completely engrossed in the role of Nick Sanders, ex-English professor turned international punching bag, that I forgot we were filming a movie. I thought I had killed a man. Just because it turns out that I didn't doesn't make the crushing guilt I felt up until only a few moments ago any less real.

"Why? Why would you feel the need to let me think that I killed you?" I ask, fighting back tears of frustration paradoxically coupled with tears of relief.

Marco pats me on the shoulder, encouraging me to let it all out as Irina unfolds a knife that appears in her hand seemingly out of nowhere.

"Don't you see, Nick? Only the persons inside this truck know that Marco is still alive. The General, Lucas Garza, and all the rest of *los hombres de la sombra*... They all now think he is dead." She enlightens as she cuts away my restraints. "And when people like that think you are dead they will instantly forget about you..."

"...and when they forget me, then they are no longer looking over their shoulder for me. Imagine all the things I can accomplish as a ghost?" Marco continuous, finishing her sentence.

Under any other circumstance I might have thought it was cute, but not today. Today it just lumps the two of them together under same category - People never invited to Thanksgiving dinner.

"Oh, how nice for you." I hiss sarcastically. "But Chase doesn't even know who you are. It's me, and now Irina, because she betrayed him. It's us he'll want dead." Emphasizing the *dead* part of my statement as audibly and succinctly as I can.

"Do not worry, *compadre. Claro que si* we must kill you both soon as well." He assures me, seemingly oblivious to tone and facial cues. "It's the only way that Chase will be out of your lives for good." He goes on, buttering me up for the inevitable catch at the end. And here it is. "But we just need you to do one last thing before you can die…"

I can't stress enough how much I hate spies. Just when you think you have the game all figured out, they pitch you another curveball that ruins your karmic batting average and distorts your perception of reality. I'm grateful Marco is alive, infinitely more grateful that I didn't kill him, even if his manipulations are the root of all my grief. But I just don't want to be here anymore. I am ready to go home, wherever that ends up being. I want to live out an insignificant life in a quiet corner of the world and struggle to write my opus. I have done enough, more than what was ever required, and I refuse to be dragged back into this spider web laid over spider's web of intrigue and mistrust…

"One last thing?" I ask incredulously, angered enough to grab Marco by the collar of his shirt and pulling him close. "You must be joking. Chase was right there. You had him dead to rights. You people messed up, not me. And still you ask for more? I'm just a retired English professor, what else could there possibly be left for me to do?"

As if on cue, the back doors of the truck swing open, bathing our impassioned little huddle in sunlight. A tall, nondescript Caucasian man in a black suit and coke bottle glasses steps out of the glare and introduces himself, his accent unplaceable yet still distinctly American.

"Hello, Professor Sanders. My name is Eddie Tor. This should explain the rest." He says curtly as he flips open his wallet to show me his CIA credentials.

From his comical name alone I am certain that this is simply another Marco misdirect, and so I immediately question the man's identity. "Eddie Tor? That sounds like a made up name." "That's because it is. "He replies, his instant admission a welcome surprise to me, although his speech inflections are so unburdened from emotion that he sounds like a robot. "The agency thought the name fitting given your former occupation." So much so that even his attempts at humor sound generated by a learning algorithm… Yes, I am a technophobe.

Know your enemy.

Agent Tor speaks with an effortless authority as if it were automatically owed to him. Despite not looking very imposing at all, the emotionless way with which her carries himself stands every hair on my body on end. If it's one thing I've learned in my many years as a teacher, no matter how cliché it may sound, it's that you should never judge a book by its cover. Take me for example, I don't look very imposing either, and I crippled a criminal empire simply by going to the public library every day.

"Hear what he has to say, Nick." Macro implores. "The *flaco hombre* is on our side."

"I'm gonna need some air if I'm going to listen to some more BS from any of you." I announce before hopping out of the back of the truck into the desert, walking around in circles as I stretch out my limbs as theatrically as possible. "What is it exactly you'd like me to do?" I finally ask when I'm good and ready. "And this time give it to me straight. No more plans within plans, within more plans, within other plans, that you all keep forgetting to loop me in on. If I smell even a hint of…"

"You are an American citizen, Professor Sanders. Rest assured that your government always has your best interests at heart." The spook reassures me, his unremarkable face completely indecipherable.

"Let's go then. Lay it on me. I'm ready now. Ask not what your country can do for you right?" I quip, knowing explicitly well that I have no choice in the matter. I either say yes to whatever he asks of me, or Marco and Irina are digging a grave in the sand to my specific dimensions.

"Your country is grateful to know that you stand with it. It will be reflected the notes." Agent Tor informs me, literally scribbling on a notepad before carrying on. "The CIA has recently come into information that suggests Chase Slate was in the process of brokering a backchannel purchase of a nuclear warhead between Belarus and Iran when he was apprehended. Unfortunately, he was allowed to escape before the warhead's specific route could be extracted from him."

I know where this is going, and I'm not exactly thrilled about it. It's nice to be needed when a colleague has had too much to drink at the annual faculty mixer and needs a ride home. It's not so nice to be needed when you have to obtain the location of a nuclear warhead from anyone.

"Chase Slate is currently in the custody of the Mexican government." Irina says as she looks up from her phone. "My man on the inside has just confirmed that he is en route to las Islas Marias."

I don't know what or where that is, but I can see that the mere mention of the place elicits a palpable response from Irina and Marco, prompting them to cross themselves twice over.

But the spooky man continues unabated. "Professor Sanders, your country calls on you to allow yourself to be imprisoned alongside Chase Slate." Dispassionately laying out the rest of his plan as if I were a decimal point on a spreadsheet. "Once there you will ingratiate yourself with him through any means at your disposal and then ascertain the whereabouts of the warhead. Assuming this approach is successful, we shall simulate a heart attack, and after a believable amount of time has passed, the prison doctor will declare you dead."

When he says it like that I almost believe it could be that easy. But when is anything ever that easy? Especially when you realize that the person who has up until now dealt in absolutes, has still resorted to an assumptions in the fine print. This has suicide mission written all over it.

But I still want him to know that I'm a patriot, so I play along. "I would be risking a lot if I agree to this." I inform the CIA automation that is coaxing me to heroism in a voice equivalent the beeping sound a car makes when it back up. "I want to intercept a nuclear warhead as much as the next guy, but why is my life less important to my country?"

"Because it just is." The man answers. Can't argue with that. Besides, I already knew I was going to agree to this two existential crisis ago. Time to iron out the details.

"But doesn't everyone think I killed him?" I point out, dipping a finger in the fake blood still pooling on Marco's shirt and flicking droplets in his face to extract some tiny form of gratification.

"And we will make sure that every inmate hears about it. A cop killer? You can't buy that kind of social currency in prison. You will be a king almost kongs." Agent Tor jokes, displaying perhaps the only hint of emotion he will ever display through a pop cultural reference of a movie from 1933.

"But what makes you think that he will ever confide in me? I argue in one last ditch effort. "The guy hates me. He's tried to have me killed more times than I have a fingers on my left hand…"

"Within the confines of a Mexican prison, the devil you know is a welcome alternative to the serial rapist that is on the top bunk." Irina asserts, sealing the deal for my incarceration…

CHAPTER 24

<u>On The Road Again</u>

I am not allowed to say goodbye to either Lauren or Ellie, even though Marco informs me my cousin has finally woken up from her head injury and is supposedly making a speedy recovery. Since I don't see it for myself, I'll just have to take his word for it. He assures me that with Chase behind bars, it is now safe for them to return to Los Osos whenever they are ready. However, since he is officially dead, Irina will be the one to personally escort them home, meeting her unfortunate end in a drunken road accident somewhere between Culiacan and Durango. Her part of this story, at least as far as Chase and his henchmen are concerned, will come to an abrupt end. While mine it seems, shall continue to go on indefinitely…

It takes two separate flights clear across the country, shackled in the deepest recesses of coach, and deprived of any in-flight entertainment, before I finally find myself at the Tepic International Airport in the Mexican state of Nayarit. The whole trip takes about half a day, passed off between one hostile federale escort to the next like the cop killing hot potatothey all believe me to be. By the end of it I am barely clinging on to a level of tired I never even thought existed.

While the flights themselves weren't absolutely terrible per say, they allowed me too much time to reflect on the latest life-threatening situation I have allowed myself to be roped into. I am not an advocate for torture under any circumstances, but it baffles me that this is the route the combined shadow governments of the United States and Mexico thought would produce the best possible outcome. It makes no sense. Why send me, a man with zero qualifications for the job, into the belly of Mexico's most notorious prison, when they could just strap Chase to a chair and pry off his fingernails until he gives up the information they need? Does he have some kind of preternatural ability to turn into a vault of secrets under extreme pressure that no-one told me about? I seriously doubt it. Everyone has a breaking point, but why are they actively searching for mine instead of his? I'm not anyone's kryptonite, and he most certainly isn't even a superman to begin with…

I don't intentionally mean to sound callous or abstruse, but hours of restless sleep and lukewarm burritos straight from an airplane microwave tend to lead a person down some very weird mental side-streets. If, as some people are prone to believe, a dream is supposed to be a glimpse into the future, then what does it mean when you cannot remember your dreams on the road to hell?

Me and my *Policía* escort, a surly fellow named Eduardo Rincon from Jalisco with a penchant for talking about something called *Chivas* in his sleep, are met by a federal transport van on the tarmac. Rincon hands me over to two uniformed guards, giving them instructions in Spanish as they usher me into the vehicle, and by usher I mean shove me inside, cuff me to a seat, and slam the door.

Unsurprisingly, I am the lone passenger. But the two guards, whom I have affectionately dubbed Heckle and Jeckle in my mind, prove to be rather congenial, dare I even say outright chatty. They must not have gotten the nationwide memo from Lucas Garza. Blasting music that they inform me is by the greatest band in the world, a Mexican rock band called Maná, they drive me from the airport directly to the San Blas pier, where the subject of the song, a woman by the name of Rebeca Méndez Jiménez, waited for 41 years for her fiancé to come back from a fishing trip.

He never made it back in case you were wondering, or so the song purports. But listening to the easy-going yet wistful tune, I can't help but stare out the heavily tinted windows and wonder how long it will take me to make it back from all of this, and if anyone will feel so strongly about my absence to write a song about it if I don't?

San Blas is apparently a popular tourist destination, well known for its surfing and birder culture, making for maybe the two most unlikely kinds of people thrown together by geography ever. Much like Chase and I are about to become as soon as I set foot on the island prison that was supposedly shut down years ago due to the numerous human rights abuses perpetrated there.

Heckle helps me out of the van and leads me down to the wharf. And as I stand out on the dock, my wrists bound together with chains, I look out at an island ominously shrouded in fog in the distance. I think back on Agent Tor's words, his paltry attempt at whimsy when bringing up King Kong becoming frighteningly too apt as I step onto the ferry that will take me to Skull Island, where I must find a way to befriend a giant ape that tramples everything in its path.

CHAPTER 25

<u>A Sojourn in Hell</u>

I have never been to a prison before, I didn't even go with my dad when he went to bail my uncle out of airport jail that one time he was detained in Newark for sneaking six jars of my Nanna's Fenek stew into the country. But if all the collective TV shows that I accidentally stumbled upon at one in the morning on basic cable have prepared me for anything, it certainly wasn't for this.

Everywhere I look, men tattooed from their foreheads to their pinkie toes with what I can only assume are their favorite cartoon characters, glare at me from behind the chainlink fence as I join the rest of the new inmates in a line in front of a pair of ironclad doors. As the prisoners on the other side of the nearly 20 foot tall fence jeer and holler menacingly at seemingly me in particular, I must admit that I have never been more glad to only have a rudimentary grasp of Spanish than I am at this precise moment, their promises of bodily harm and sexual assault blunted by ignorance.

During the first phase of processing I am ordered to surrender my personal effects to an apathetic man sitting behind a glass enclosure similar to what you would find at the DMV. But since my passport and wallet were confiscated before I even got on the first airplane, I have nothing to slip through the mouth of his window besides a packet of airplane peanuts and some used wet wipes.

During the second phase another indifferent man takes my fingerprints while I am asked standard questions like my name and date of birth, but also some truly macabre ones like 'Have you, now or ever, had a desire to consume human flesh?', which above anything else, makes me extremely wary of the kind of people that are locked up in here. The human brain is a truly wondrous contraption, at least mine is, suppressing my existential dread through the use of highly facetious verbiage. Once I am finished with the processing stage, the guards lead me into a grimy shower room with cracked tiles and free-range cockroaches. They then strip me naked, dousing me in some kind of citrus-smelling white powder before blasting me against the wall with a handheld water cannon. I have never felt cleaner nor more violated in my entire life. As I lay there on the wet floor, curled up in a fetal position to cover up all my delicate bits as a heavyset woman dries me with a leaf blower,

I know that I will never be able to experience a carwash quite the same way again…

Once I am dry I am given a uniform to put on - heavily starched white pants with a blue stripe down the leg and a polyester white shirt bearing my inmate number on the back - a guard takes me and the rest of my motley group into a room the size of a racquetball court. It is here in this holding area, all of us piled together like livestock before the slaughter, that the chieftain of skull island decides to address us. He is an unimposing man, on the verge of timid, with a look and demeanor more in line with a zookeeper than the warden of an island prison housing the country's most violent offenders.

His words, delivered with the cadence of an underpaid high school history teacher, are short and succinct: This island is in the middle of shark infested waters. There is no escape. Don't even try.

After the warden's cordial and threat-laced warning, the ancillary gate swings open as if on cue. The guards parades us through the prison yard, down a veritable no man's land of disputed territory carved out between rival gangs through blood, sweat and provisional jailhouse commerce; where scary men of all shapes and sizes are doing surprisingly mundane things like playing soccer while simultaneously behind the back dealing in illicit substances. But in my head all I see are a horde of cannibals sharpening their machetes on ad hoc whetstones, all too eager to lop off one of my limbs for an afternoon snack the moment I even look at them sideways. Yet despite this illuminating case study of a failure-bound experiment in mass incarceration I currently find myself participating in, it's what comes next that actually makes me regret agreeing to do this…

CHAPTER 26
El Diablo Blanco

The ghost of Deb is suddenly walking beside me, whispering cat poster quotes of encouragement in my ear in a nondescript Central-California coastal accent as I am led to my cell. I do not question the apparition and instead let it envelop me like armor. As long as she is with me in spirit while I cower through the valley of the shadow of death, then I shall at least try not to fear no evil as much as a rational-minded person like myself probably should. Edmund Dantes was stuck on an island hell hole for fourteen years and came out on the other side quite wealthy, if somewhat bitter and just a tad vengeful. I do not plan to be here for even a fraction of that length of time, in fact I was assured that this whole thing would take the better part of a week. Then again, those assurances are predicated on my untested capability to appeal to Chase's better angels and extract the route of a doomsday weapon currently in the hands of doomsday-inclined people who want to watch the world burn. It's a tall order for a man humbled daily by advancing age and grappling to come to terms with his own mediocrity. But I required nothing short of excellence from all my students, and I in turn I owe it to them not to flinch from greatness when that same uncompromising and exacting mirror has now been turned in my general direction.

With a lumpy pillow and a moth-eaten blanket neatly folded in my arms, I arrive at the entrance to a six by eight foot windowless concrete shoebox and come face to face once again with the Lord Byron to my John Keats, the Brahms to my Tchaikovsky, the Monday to my Garfield. A huge part of me was skeptical that Marco would be able to deliver on even this initial part of the plan, but there Chase is as promised, leaning against the wall of the top bunk and casually flipping through a Spanish translation of an old Archie & Reggie double digest. "No estoy de humor, Papá Pitufo." Chase says with a distinctly peninsular Spanish accent, not bothering to take his eyes off his comic book. "Ya te lo dije, Elizabeth Taylor murió hace años."

"Did you really know Elizabeth Taylor or is that just another one of your many lies?" I ask as I enter the cell, using the question as a way to announce myself, yet also genuinely curious about whether or not he actually had a relationship with a childhood crush of mine.

Chase's slowly looks up at the sound of an American voice, and like a shark tasting blood in the water, a huge smile breaking across his face as soon as he sees that the voice belongs to me.

"Of course I did." He answers matter-of-factly, and I'm inclined to believe him. "She was a magnificent creature. The purple rose of Cairo that swore like a sailor right up until the end."

He sets the comic book down and swings his legs over the edge, intentionally dangling his slip-on sandals in front of my face as I busy myself with setting my prison issued toiletry on the stained mattress below his. "Of all the cells, in all the island prisons in all the world…" He begins with no small amount of amusement, wasting no time getting under my skin. "And the heroic professor walks into mine. I don't know whether to laugh at this auspicious turn of events or take the opportunity to punch you in the face."

Annoyed, I snatch one of his sandals and toss it out of the cell. When he climbs down from his bunk I stand in his way, refusing to budge as he tries to squeeze past me while hoping on one leg. If you're going to give in to pettiness in the first place then you might as well do it properly right?

"I'd like to see you try, Chase. I really would." I challenge him, practically begging him to take a swing at me, looking for any excuse to throw the entire plan out the window for a chance to wipe the grind of his face with one well-placed shot to his mouth. "I'm right here. Take your best shot."

Seeing the undeniable fire raging in my eyes, Chase backs down, leaving his slipper where it lies for the time being. "Or maybe I'll just get someone in here to do it. I can have one of these thugs slit your throat in the showers for a handful of loose cigarettes and a mid-priced beach house in Belize."

"I doubt that." I answer defiantly, refusing to be intimidated anymore. "The fact that you're threatening me instead of just going ahead and doing it means you do not have that kind of influence here. Not yet anyway…"

Chase clings on to his enmity for a few more seconds before sighing in frustration, effectively conceding my point. He plunks down right on top of my toiletries, his weight popping the cap off my tube of toothpaste and sending its contents spurting out all over my mattress. Even in defeat he still manages to find away to make my life just a little more messy and uncomfortable.

"You're not wrong. I must admit that it has been somewhat difficult getting in touch with my people from in here." He unexpectedly confesses, his overall demeanor reminding me of a sulking ten year old whining about being deprived of all his toys.

"I never though I'd see the day. You've been neutered. The General did his job well." I proclaim gleefully, looking down at a powerful man battered humble and enjoying the view immensely.

"You can't still be this naive, Professor Sanders!" He blurts out while laughing at me incredulously. "The General is an old fool… Nothing more than a minor piece on the chessboard. A secondary character in the elaborate stage play of global politics with an eye on the staring role. I am in this deep dark hole with you, not by his hand, but by the hands that force it. Make no mistake, I have been trapped here for one reason, and one reason alone."

"And what reason might that be?" I ask, not entirely sure that I want to know the answer. But his allusions to a greater force at play have piqued my interest. And as I have unfortunately proven since that fateful night in Los Osos, I will always be a dog with a bone chasing cars on the freeway.

"Don't you find it odd that I wasn't immediately extradited back to the U.S.?" He asks, holding my full attention in the palm of his hand. A skilled orator coaxing the audience into participation.

"As I understand it, you've pissed the world off, Chase. But since Mexico caught you, Mexico gets to punish you." I answer, but with much less conviction than I would like.

"Wrong." He quickly declares, eager to illuminate me yet clearly finding no pleasure in it. And as he spells it all out, I realize that I have become his personal sin-eater. "You took me off the board, Professor. Power hates a vacuum. Over 2,000 years ago, after Alexander the Great's sudden death, his Diadochi couldn't agree on who would take his place. They fought epic battles until his empire was carved up between them and became a shadow of its former glory. That's what is happening now. I am in here as leverage because your good friend the General wants a bigger piece of the pie that I baked. But you see, so does everyone else. And they will wage devastating wars against each other until only one man is left standing to take my place in the kitchen."

An electronic horn suddenly blares out, fuzzy and jarring, but I am far too overwhelmed by the information that Chase has just unburdened on me to truly hear it. And so when he stands up, I am not actually sure why.

"Where are you going?" I ask, confused and disoriented, my heart beating so fast that it hurts.

"That's the lunch bell." Chase informs me. "I hope you like eating cardboard. I've found that it does wonders for my digestion. I haven't had a bowel movement since I got here…"

CHAPTER 27
The Escape goats

"I know why they sent you here, Professor." Chase says as we sit across from each other in the tightly packed prison cafeteria, a place of bolted picnic tables and dehumanizing social hierarchy not much different from the one at my old high school.

"Why did they send me here, Chase?" I ask, nervously prodding at the assortment of foul smelling pig slop on my plate with a plastic spork.

"You're here because your handlers want to know where the warhead I sold those Arabs is. Wait, was it the Arabs or was it the Basque?" Chase asks me, sounding genuinely unable to recall.

"Persians." I correct him without looking up, still transfixed by the complex ecosystem on my plate that is currently evolving and gaining sentience right before my eyes.

"The Persians. Of course. Sorry. I've sold so many nasty weapons to so many unsavory people over the years that I've lost count... Keeping the world destabilized and malleable takes its toll on a man I suppose." He says, his nonchalance reminding me that he is no longer an actual person but rather a patchwork monster stapled together with decades of callous arrogance and delinquent habits.

"Poor you." I retort sarcastically, secretly chastising myself for once allowing him too much of my awe and ardor. And to think that I once pitied him. The untimely loss of a good woman should never, and can never, be anyone's excuse for world domination.

"They must really be desperate if they think that *you* of all people might succeed where much better men have failed." Chase taunts, and while his words have a tendency to set me off when I least expect it, this doesn't seem to be one of those times.

"There is no more *they*, Chase. Just *us*. Just me and you. And I'm promise you that I'm going to get that information one way or another." I state as calmly and clearly as I can, letting him know that I mean business without crossing over into explicitness. But as a flicker of fear flashes on his face, I learn that there is room for menace between the fixed margins of perspicuousness.

"No need for threats, Professor. I'll tell you what you want to know. You'll be taking that information to your grave soon enough." He says as his voice falters, suddenly shifting uncomfortably in his seat while his eyes dart around the cafeteria.

"What is that supposed to mean?" I ask while trying to ascertain what exactly it is he is looking for. And it dawns on me that it isn't me that he's afraid of.

"You'll see." He says, craning his neck over his shoulder until he abruptly stops, looking straight at me with vacant eyes, a dog listening for something on a frequency only it's aware of. "You hear that?

"I don't hear anything." I admit after a while, yet my body stiffens as it reacts to the palpable tension in the air. I instinctively know that something is about to happen, and I am once again afraid.

"Exactly. The birds are gone. Get ready. They're coming…" Chase warns me ominously before an explosion rocks the entire prison, sending debris and inmates flying in every direction.

A chunk of concrete strikes me across the face and my knees immediately buckle. I crumple to the floor, fighting desperately to stay conscious on the way down, but some things are just inevitable. My life flashes before my eyes as I tumble deeper into the void, the first time this has ever happened to me despite the countless times that my life has been in danger. But I do not accept the slideshow of my greatest hits and force my eyes open. I awake to find that I am laying facedown in a puddle of my lunch, my ears ringing, breathing in the the mystery meat pressed against my cheek. I may not know what is going on, but I do know that I can't stay prone like this.

It takes longer than I would like, but I eventually will my limbs into action, digging deep within myself and summoning the strength to push against the floor and lift myself up off the ground.

I look around, but my vision is the equivalent of an old television with bad reception, the screen snowy and the images garbled. One thing is clear though, there is daylight flooding through a massive hole in the cafeteria wall, creating a spotlight on a man dressed head to toe in black tactical body armor pointing his machine gun at a kneeling Chase.

A part of me knows that life would be so much simpler for the entire world if I just let this presumed assassin pull the trigger and end everything that is Chase once and for all. But then there would still be a warhead floating around in the ether, an unknown quantity, a cat in a box that could or could not be used to slaughter millions…

A tug of war breaks out inside my head, a struggle between my two brains unfolding over milliseconds. When the choice is between two angels, which angel's wings do you choose to clip?

In times of indecision such as these, the thing you are expected to do is to trust your gut. Which is not a conclusion that I come to naturally. But I do understand commitment, despite what my ex-wife may tell you. I was sent here to do something, and it's something that could potentially prove to be the most important thing that anyone has ever done in the history of mankind. It's okay to wobble on the tracks from time to time, just as long as you never allow yourself to be derailed…

I stand, my body bloodied and bent, and kick out with all my might. My foot hits the barrel of the gun just as the assassin pulls the trigger, forcing it to the side so that the bullet intended for his forehead only nicks Chase's ear.

I collapse right after, no longer able to keep myself upright. The assassin stands over me, his feelings about my intervention concealed behind a stoic mask, but his intentions are soon made clear when he points the gun down at me. Chase comes to my rescue, taking the knife sheathed in the assassin's boot and stabbing the man in the thigh, twisting it in half-circles for savage measure. Chase picks me up off the ground while the assailant writhes in pain, his screams muffled by the thick cloth of his balaclava. Once I am back upright, I see that there are other men dressed exactly the same as Chase's assassin inside the prison, but thankfully they are too busy fending off the other inmates to pay us any attention as we hobble to the hole in the wall.

Chase and I stand there, the salty sea breeze ruffling our hair as we stare down at the waves crashing against the rocks below. The cosmos is asking a lot of me right now, propped up by my sworn enemy, the only escape from certain death being a hundred foot drop into freezing waters. We look at each other, incapacitated by our mutual distrust. But the decision is taken out of our hands when the assailant, the knife still jammed into his thigh like Excalibur, slams against Chase and sends all three off us plummeting over the edge…

AN EPILOGUE
The Deep Blue Nothing –

Another sun sets on an endless, sparkling ocean. Chase and I are still drifting along aimlessly with the current, clutching for dear life to a prison cafeteria table made slightly more buoyant by the dead body of a would-be assassin that we have strapped underneath it.

"Are we still going in the wrong direction, Nick?" Chase asks through chattering teeth, his lips severely chapped from exposure to the elements.

"We're drifting towards the sunset again, and that means land is behind us, so yeah, Chase, I'd say we're still going in the wrong direction." I answer irritably, although I am too exhausted to fully intonate my annoyance at being asked this for the hundredth time…

Call me Professor Nick Sanders. Some days ago—how long precisely no longer matters—having little or no choice at my disposal, and evading certain death on an island prison at the hands of highly skilled assassins sent to kill the notorious criminal floating beside me, I thought I would drift about a little on a bloating corpse on the fringes of the Pacific Ocean with my sworn enemy…

But as the day ends and another pitch-black night threatens my sanity, the orange sun dunks itself into the sea once more, only this time it reveals a shape on the horizon…

I notice it first, a triangular silhouette cruising across the water in the distance. My heart skips a beat, allowing hope to flood in during the intermittence.

"Hey, do you see that?" Chase asks with, still able muster up some excitement after all these days pruning in the ocean. "Am I hallucinating or is that the sail of a boat?"

"I'm not sure. It seems to be moving awfully fast." I answer, observing the triangular shape as it effortlessly cuts through the water, gasping loudly as I watch it abruptly change course and head in directly toward us…

Is this the end for Nick and Chase? Tune in next time to

find out…